ONLINE

OR OFF

ONLINE

OR OFF

BITTY COLLINS

CAROLYN JAXSON

FIRST EDITION

Printed in the United States of America

Cover design by Mary King-Moore and Teresa Heidt

Author photo courtesy: Nicole Hudson

ISBN-13: 9798688921557

ACKNOWLEDGEMENTS

Our second novel is definitely a labor of love and could not have been completed without the support of our family and friends. We would especially like to thank Lemmy and Jaxson for providing much needed sustenance. Wine, margaritas, chips and queso kept us in the zone. Anita, Jessica, Valerie, and KPH thank you for reading our first draft and providing such valuable feedback. Nicole, thank you for your photography skills and making us look so good. Many thanks for the continued support of our retail friends. This year we have seen the retail world change dramatically and are thankful for the experiences it has brought us which led to the HeidtMoore series.

PROLOGUE

The ice sparkles in the blazing sunlight. A blistering wind cuts through, strong enough to break frozen tree limbs, if there were any to break. The land is baron, nothing but ice and black soil on the dry earth. It is a hostile environment. The bitter chill of Antarctica makes it impossible for humans to survive in such extreme conditions. But for the penguin, it is an ideal place. The black and white flightless birds waddle along in groups, like a pack of tuxedoed waiters at an upscale restaurant waiting around for the last table to finish their meal.

Crackling shards break off into the deep blue sea, causing one of the birds to lose its balance and slide towards the edge of the icy cliff. The others pay no attention and continue their mission to find food and shelter. Should one bird leave the flock it would be devastation for the pack, who travel far distances in unison. But luckily for this little penguin he quickly catches up with the others, flipping its wings rapidly to gain speed.

While all seems serene in this frozen landscape, there lies a great threat, lingering close to the water's edge. It's the leopard seal. One of the most formidable hunters in Antarctica, with incredibly powerful jaws. He cruises the edge waiting for one of the birds to dive in in search of food. It is only a matter of time. If the birds are to survive, they need to outpace the hunter and keep moving forward. They slow down and begin their descent into the frigid waters. This is the moment the seal has been waiting for. He launches his whole body out of the sea and clenches his jaws on one of the smaller birds. SNAP! Nothing remains other than a few black feathers floating in air. Without any time to waste the colony of birds moves away from the scene and must now look for another source of food.

GOOD MORNING

Beep. Beep. Beep beep.

Mary rolled to her side pulling the covers up trying to stay warm. She woke up feeling extraordinarily cold, her teeth chattering. It was so cold she didn't want to get out of bed to check the air conditioning. Instead, Mary opened one eye and glanced towards the alarm clock brightly blinking 5:30 a.m. She rolled back over onto her other side and nestled deeply in the warm covers not wanting to get out, let alone get ready for a run. She dozed off for another minute, her mind going back to the frozen tundra.

"Good morning Mary it's 5:35 a.m."

Mary opened one eye again and glanced over to the Alexa speaker sitting on the bookshelf in her bedroom. The speaker was now playing the song *"Cold"*, by Maroon 5. *Very coincidental*, Mary thought.

"Alexa turn off music," whispered Mary feeling incredibly groggy. The music continued to play. Alexa not having heard Mary's command.

"Alexa! Turn off the music," she said, a little louder.

Once again, Mary pushed her head under the covers, hoping to get another few minutes of sleep.

A moment later, her Fitbit watch started beeping at the exact moment her Apple TV turned on with the local news. *Why couldn't she just sleep a little longer?*

It was retail business reporter, Linda Langley on the local news announcing a cold front headed to Dallas for the weekend.

"An unusual cold front will be hitting Dallas. Expect to see temperatures fall dramatically over the next week or so. Will this be a driver for retailers? Only time will tell. But one thing's for sure, you'll want to dress up warm folks! Bye for now. Linda Langley, reporting from channel eight local news."

Mary made it a habit to listen to the news every morning for the latest retail updates. *Unbelievable.* It was mid-August. Way too early for Texas to be getting a cold front! Mary sighed and decided it was time to get out of bed. Her long days at the HeidtMoore department store were exhausting.

Thank goodness she exhibited her organizational habits even at home. Mary had placed her running shorts and tank top on the chair beside her bed the night before. Shoes and socks were there also. She barely needed to open her eyes to get dressed. Scuffling slowly to the bathroom she brushed her teeth and put in her contacts. *Ah, now I can see!* She was as blind as a bat and it had been that way since Mary was eight years old.

Noticing her messy hair, she gave it a good brush and tossed it into a hot pink 1980s clippie. She was aiming for that cool, not trying too-hard look, a la Hailey Bieber. Cool and understated. She fixed her bun just so, giving the impression she hadn't done much, where in reality, it took her a good fifteen minutes to get the bun just right. She was determined to make a good impression. She carefully made up her face. Not too much makeup, just enough to cover a few blemishes and highlight her large almond eyes. She dusted her face with Estée Lauder shimmer powder. Perfect! Mary laughed to herself, looking in the mirror. To achieve the popular 'makeup free' look, which was the latest trend amongst millennials, it had taken Mary twice as long to do her makeup than normal. She used three different beige concealers to get the look she was going for, all thanks to a Kim Kardashian 'how to get a makeup-free look' tutorial she had found on YouTube. Once she was satisfied with her appearance she went back to the bedroom and grabbed her ear buds and phone and headed downstairs to the kitchen.

Mary had only been in her apartment for a few months. She had finally saved enough money to move out on her own, leaving her mom and brother, Samson, to fend for themselves. She had only moved a few minutes away from her childhood home which put her closer to work. The apartment was a small two-bedroom, one bathroom, with a charming living area, kitchen, and garage. The downstairs living area was sparsely furnished, with a couch she had purchased from Wayfair online and chairs, which were a lucky find at an estate sale in Highland Park, one of the wealthiest neighborhoods in Dallas. One thing was missing. She still had not found the perfect kitchen table, so for now it was simply a card table that had been used as a visual prop at work. One day after work she found the perfectly usable table by a dumpster on the way back to her car. Deciding not to let a good thing go to waste, Mary hauled it back to her apartment.

Upstairs, her bedroom was quaintly decorated with a mix of furniture from Pottery Barn, Target, Ikea, and of course the HeidtMoore 'Half of Half' sale. A few pictures of her mom and her brother Samson and some friends were placed about the room. It was a simple space. The only place in the apartment Mary had invested in was the Cloffice, her own little piece of heaven. Mary had turned the second bedroom into a closet and an office, aptly named the Cloffice. Both closets in the bedrooms were strictly for shoes. The Cloffice, bordered with hanging rods and was filled with clothes. Since working at the HeidtMoore, Mary had acquired a nice collection of designer clothes. She had Marie Kondo'd the place from the beginning, everything was loved, brought her joy, and had its own special place. One end of the room had a mirror and antique vanity that her mother had given her. In the center of the room was a desk, flanked by chairs with her computer, some books, and files. In one corner of the room there was another lounge chair and a round ottoman. The other end of the room had two floor-to-ceiling shelves for handbags, folded sweaters, and accessories. It had taken several months to complete the Cloffice, but she adored this room. She really loved her apartment and living on her own.

Eyes barely open, she made her way to the kitchen and opened the refrigerator. As much as she hated to admit it, she missed the morning routine of waking up to a fully cooked breakfast prepared by her mom, Deloris.

"Mi amore, your eggy peggy is ready." Deloris would say.

She sure wished she had that eggy peggy now. Mary felt dazed as she opened the bare refrigerator; a yogurt, a few old strawberries, a bit of sliced turkey, a Chinese take-out box and a container containing God knows what. Mary didn't remember. *Maybe it's time I throw that out. Gross.* She thought to herself.

Just as she was about to grab the container, her phone beeped. She looked to see who it was and closed the refrigerator door, forgetting to throw out the food in the process.

Bing. Bing.

She walked over to her granite kitchen countertop to see who the message was from.

It was Nacho.

"On my way to the dog park," the text message read.

Her heart skipped a beat.

It was time.

RUNNING BEHIND

Nacho and Mary met for the first time the day she got the job at the HeidtMoore. He was the head of the security team and took his job very seriously. He had not had a girlfriend in quite some time and was surprised at how attracted he was to Mary. Their relationship started last spring when they went to retrieve a missing handbag, for one of the stores top customers, Mrs. Ivory.

Nacho made it to the dog park by 6:00 a.m. the morning of the run and was already fully stretched and ready to go. He was planning a nice, easy 10k. Easy for him, not so easy for others…like Mary. But true to form, not wanting to admit she couldn't do it, Mary agreed to the long run. Yikes! What had she got herself into?!

Mary pulled up and parked next to Nacho's black GMC truck. She took a moment, looked down at her Apple watch and hit the one-minute breathing app, "Breathe". She thought it might calm her nerves and focus her energy. It did the job. Thankfully. She got out of her car and walked towards her running date. If this were a *'date'* Mary would need to make sure that, in the future, Nacho might just take her to dinner or see a movie. That would work fine. But no, on their first "active" outdoors date, here they were, about to go on an epic run, in August. *August in Texas!* Thank goodness for the cold front! Mary had not run in over a year and was really feeling very out of shape and very self-conscious. It wasn't that she was overweight or unfit. The HeidtMoore certainly made sure the employees had an ample amount of exercise running around all day seeing to one customer's need or another. She just wasn't particularly athletic that's all. And now, she had led Nacho to believe she could run all over the city!

"Awesome! You ready? I'm pumped," he said as he put one arm over his head, while his other hand reached across to hold the opposite elbow.

Mary could barely say a word. She had never seen Nacho in tight shorts and sleeveless athletic top before. His muscles were bulging in every direction. It was the way he looked like Vin Diesel that simply made Mary swoon. He sort of…glowed.

Mary so hoped she also glowed. The thought of running alongside this stallion made Mary want to look her best. In order to hide the giant drops of perspiration she imagined would be dripping down her face, she strategically brushed "glow" translucent powder, across her face and chest. It gave Mary a natural, if very sparkling, glowing appearance.

After Mary performed a few lame stretches, barely able to touch her toes, she was ready. It was now or never. *What had she gotten herself into?*

"I'm ready," Mary lied.

Off they ran.

About four minutes into the run, Mary was exhausted and as red as a lobster. This was a terrible idea, but she couldn't give up now.

They ran through the large leafy dog park, ran through downtown, ran across a school field, and ran up onto a designated running path called The Katy Trail. This was a popular trail in Dallas. By this time Mary thought she would die! Along the way, Nacho told her all about his dreams to run the Great Wall of China. *Was he crazy?* Distracted by his conversation, she was doing pretty well keeping up. She even shocked herself when she looked at her watch to discover she had already covered 3.5 miles. Mary had never achieved that in her life. But there was still an additional 2.5 to go. She was exhausted and trying extremely hard not to show it.

She could taste the glow powder trickling down her face and into her mouth. *Yuck!* She noticed runners running towards them who seemed to be running off course, squinting their eyes in the process. Mary couldn't understand what was wrong with them. It didn't occur to her that it may have something to do with her makeup. The sparkle of the powder caught the sun's light, literally leaving a "blinding" impression.

"So, Mary, what are your goals in life?" Nacho asked, as they started running along a creek. Mary was trying her best to keep up with Nacho. The creek was tranquil and surrounded by gorgeous mansions. This proved to be a great distraction for Mary as they ran.

"Well, I want to move up in the company." *Pant, pant.* Mary was so out of breath it was hard to talk. "I'd like...to...stay working...in fashion, maybe as a...buyer. I used to want to work for a magazine..." Now she was huffing and puffing.

"That's awesome. You'd be great at that. Some of the buyers I've met are pretty tough though. You seem so sweet."

"I seem?" Half mocking Nacho.

He laughed. "I mean you are sweet." He gave her a gentle nudge.

Mary smiled. It gave her a little confidence boost and she felt herself running a little faster.

"You? What do you want to do?"

"Me? I have big plans. One day I'll run the HeidtMoore. This is what's going to happen..."

"Wow!" The only word she could manage as they ran up a steep incline. "That's impressive. You'll have to beat out Boggs and Sloan though. They seem to be going for that same role."

"Ha! Yeah, tell me about it. They try a little too hard if you ask me."

Nacho told Mary all about his lofty goals and how he planned to achieve his ambitions. Listening to Nacho made their time together fly by. Thankfully! Hanging on to every word he said, Mary didn't realize they had already run five miles. She never wanted to run this far ever again. *Ever.* Her legs were feeling like jelly and her thighs like cement. Her face was blotchy and red. Before the run, Mary envisioned she would look like an easy, breezy, millennial, like Haley Bieber or Selena Gomez, but now she thought she probably looked more like a flying piece of salmon.

The sun was shining high in the sky and the temperature already rising. The last half mile felt like running three all over again. But Mary was determined to finish. With every fiber of her body, she was determined to finish the damn run.

She did it. She had finished the run and was completely out of breath. Finally, she had done it. The run was over. Of course, Nacho looked as if he had barely broken a sweat. *How on earth had he accomplished that?* Mary felt she was sweating for the both of them. She was so hot and her T-shirt was dripping, soaking wet, but...she had persevered AND won the respect of the man of her dreams – Nacho. That's all that mattered. He seemed eager to continue their running together. He didn't notice, or didn't care, that her makeup was smeared across her face and her hair damp from sweat.

Standing by a lamppost, she held onto it to steady herself. Not knowing if she would faint or not, it took a moment for her to catch her breath.

"You good?" Asked Nacho, who obviously had made a full recovery.

"Yep. Yep. I'm good." A complete lie.

"Let's do this again! Next week?"

"Yes! Let's do it!" Mary responded a little too quickly. It must be love.

SUMMER SUMMARY

Back at the store, summer was winding down, and customers were beginning to shop again. Thank goodness. Business had been very tough. Except for the online business, that is. Online was killing it and had been exceeding sales goals by 300% to plan - much to the dismay of the associates who wanted all the sales to happen in the store.

It was always a struggle to sell during the summer months. This year had been particularly bad, despite coming off of a great Spring season. The past spring had seen an unprecedented increase in store sales, primarily due to the well-attended personal appearance by the Hollywood duo, Hudson Hawn. A fashion trendy mom and daughter team, Kate Hudson and Goldie Hawn. Then it became business as usual for the summer, which reached an all-time low. With not much else to do, but stand around and gossip, the associates felt like it was an eternity before they would be able to sell again and make any money.

"Wish Mrs. Dinkleheimer would hurry up and come shop."

"Where is she?"

"St. Tropez with her pool boy."

"Some people have all the luck."

Typical floor gossip during the summer months.

During the hottest months of the year, June through September, the HeidtMoore was like a ghost town. The customers left Dallas for trips abroad, cooler places like Aspen, or to their second homes on the west coast, like Napa, and to the Hamptons, on the east coast. The atmosphere in the store was so different as compared to the hustle and bustle of the typical fall season.

Associates also had to adjust to sweeping technology changes taking over the department store. Fortunately, most of the selling associates had acclimated to the electronic clientele books, but there were still some who felt a dramatic change in their business since they refused to adapt to the digital age. They would rather stick to the old ways of doing business, like writing down account numbers on loose pieces of paper, to be stored away in giant three ring binder client books. Even though each associate was told time and time again that this was illegal.

"What on earth is this?" Walking the floor one day, Sloan found a torn off piece of paper with an eight-digit number scribbled on the back and a name which read Mrs. C. Prickle. *Huh. Never heard of her,* Sloan thought to himself, before looking up to see who was around. Good thing he found the account number before a random customer did!

"Is this yours?" He asked the nearest sales associate on the sales floor, who happened to be Olga. Olga, the Russian born associate was known for her crafty ways, but she was smart enough not to lose anything like a customer's account number and would certainly never scribble it down on a random piece of paper.

"Mine? No, never see it, in my life. What you think I am? Stupid?"

"No, that's not what I am saying. Of course not." Sloan said defensively. "But I need to know who or why someone would do this? We could get into a lot of trouble. This is serious, Olga."

Sloan put the piece of paper in his coat pocket and walked away.

"Don't worry, I'll go and shred this."

Aside from the occasional written account, the ancient way of jotting down notes in the large and bulky client books was now, for the most part, a thing of the past. All the information was now stored online and all messages to customers were electronic. Each associate had the

11

customers purchase history and spending level and knew exactly what they had been browsing online. All was in the palm of the hands of the associates with the company supplied phones. The HeidtMoore tech team named the software *I-Snoop*.

The members of the executive team intended to get the store as well as the associates in tip top shape before the onset of the fall season. For Sloan Garret and Boggs Daniel, the Assistant Store Managers, it was not only imperative to the store's success, but also in order to fulfill their ambitions of becoming the store's next General Manager.

In order to keep the HeidtMoore running smoothly, the plan was to have the associates spend the early part of summer sending pictures to their customers of sale items. Then, the last part of the summer the associates were to entice the customers into securing new fall product, such as furs and boots as soon as they became available for sale. The "million-dollar books", as they were known, were in fact the sales associates who sold over a million dollars each season. These million-dollar books had selling down to an art and kept busy year-round. But to the majority of associates, the vision set forth by the executive team was not working. These associates didn't care anymore and were feeling uninspired.

Regardless of the time of year, and what the associates were doing to drive their business, the managers of HeidtMoore were always busy. If they weren't methodically planning out how to overachieve sales goals for the season ahead, they were constantly preaching to the associates, reminding them also to plan for the future. The motto was, "Talk less, reach new *Heidts* and sell *Moore*."

August was the time of year when vendors from around the world descended upon Dallas' trendy hotels and hosted the HeidtMoore buying teams. The vendors debuted the new collections for the fall season. The 'Lifers', the managers who had been with the HeidtMoore for more than 15 years, loved this time of year to get re-acquainted with the buyers and to get the first peek at what was coming along for the highly anticipated holiday season. For the managers who had special relationships with these buyers, it also meant receiving all sorts of gifts. Sarafina, had one year, acquired an exquisite aquamarine a one of a kind Coomi broach. Mary and the other relatively new managers were able to use the time to finally put faces to the names on emails and text messages they received the previous season. In fact, Mary had met some of the buyers during the Hudson Hawn personal appearance. These buyers all come out of the woodwork and show up in the department store for any event where celebrities may be present.

These buying events, or conclaves as they were called, were glamorous events. They were held in the most distinguished hotels in town and featured the best designers, showcasing their latest exciting collections. The managers and buyers would all receive swag from each vendor. Free merchandise and samples of nearly every product carried in the HeidtMoore would be left in each manager's hotel room. Knowing this, most of them brought two empty suitcases to the hotel in order to carry all of the freebies home after the meetings and runway shows. The evening agendas consisted of fabulous cocktail parties and 5-star dining experiences from restaurants all over the city.

It was at one of these conclaves that a famed designer tragically overdosed at one of the after parties. The HeidtMoore capitalized on the tragic event and ended up selling an outstanding two hundred and fifty-two units in one week, resulting in the company's two percent increase.

Some of the vendors hosted HeidtMoore managers at their showrooms in various cities throughout the world. It was not uncommon for managers to spend a long weekend in Italy, viewing the Brunello Cucinelli muted color palettes in the most exquisite fabrics. After the stop in Italy they jet off to Canada to visit the fur showroom of Leonard Gorski. Gorski Furs had the finest assembly of minks, chinchillas, and sables in the world.

Unfortunately, all good things do come to an end. Over the last couple of years, the HeidtMoore started cutting budgets, which meant no more stays at the likes of a Ritz Carlton and no more unlimited expense accounts. All vendors, buyers and managers had to stay elsewhere and make other plans. Could they stay in the luxurious accommodations of years past? No. Now everyone stayed at the Holiday Inn. Not a happy situation for many.

13

"This is like, so, like, awful," said an assistant handbag buyer named Chloe entering her suite at the Doves Inn, a local motel located in south Dallas, mostly used by truck drivers.

Yes. The company was in dire straits.

"Like, omg. People actually stay here?" She said to Miranda, a Precious Jewelry buyer who had been with the HeidtMoore since graduating college back in the late 1960's.

"Oh darling, put on an eye mask and go to sleep."

"You think this is ok? Like, gross. I'm afraid to put my YSL handbag down on anything in this room." Chloe was mortified by the plastic laminate that covered every surface of the small motel room she was forced to share with her colleague. It didn't help that Miranda, the buyer for Couture, was so much older than Chloe and was always condescending and out of touch. What did she know?

Miranda had already dropped her bag, a Prada exotic, and she had started unpacking her suitcase. In no time, she had her La Mer face mask on and was pulling back the nylon bed covers to one of the two single beds in the room. The very fact that everyone had to "double up" simply appalled Chloe, who didn't even have a roommate in college.

When Chloe graduated from Tulane, a year prior to joining the HeidtMoore, she didn't know what she would do with her degree in art history. Ideally, she would not join the workforce and instead marry her high school sweetheart, Roger Buckley. She would stay at home and attend charity functions for causes she cared little about. Maybe she would have two children, probably not any more than two, because she heard horror stories about trying to get rid of the weight gain and it wasn't pretty. No, two was the right number. Of course, she would make Roger see to a personal trainer in their prenup.

In reality, marriage was not in the cards anytime soon. Roger decided that he would move to San Diego for a job at Dropbox. Chloe was devastated but determined to make a go of it and show him she could stand on her own two Manolo covered feet.

Despite all odds, the past spring season had been a successful one. With the store sales exceeding sales plans by 5%. Not bad. This was particularly good given all the troubles the HeidtMoore had encountered; the active shooter (who was caught thankfully), a black out that shut off all the registers during one of the most highly anticipated promotional events, the case of the missing emerald necklace, and internal computer systems failing.

Then there was the shock of Mr. Heidt, the revered store manager's apparent sudden death. When the news of Mr. Heidt's death spread through every department like wildfire, some felt certain this would be the end of the store. No one could really believe he had died or could settle on what actually happened to him. But everyone knew the store would not survive long without him.

The HeidtMoore needed serious repair. The gold was unpolished, and the fixtures were dated. The fluorescent lights flickered in areas throughout the store and the store morale was at an all-time low. To make matters worse, even the huge gold block letters that read "HEIDTMOORE", hanging above the entrance to the store, was looking worse for wear. The 'H' was ever so slightly tilted. Almost like a metaphor for its interior…barely hanging on.

In a move to make brick and mortar more viable and compete with online, the once grand department store had neglected the very thing that made the HeidtMoore so famous – its appearance. Like the Roman colosseum after the fall of the empire, the HeidtMoore would soon be on its way to dust and rubble, especially it it did not have a General Manager to oversee everything during the busiest time of year.

If the HeidtMoore was going to survive, the Fall season would need to be one to remember.

HEADED TO WORK

Stopping at the red light, Mary grabbed her phone and opened the Starbucks app. This was her daily routine en route to work, and she quickly hit the re-order button before the light changed. Mary requested her morning chai tea latte from the Starbucks down the road from work. She had this down to a science and usually received at least one a week free of charge because of the points she had accrued. It was a huge amount of money that Mary could not afford, but she needed that fix to get her through the day.

Mary parked near the employee entrance of the HeidtMoore, three floors above street level and got out of her car. In the little, light blue, Mini Cooper, parked right beside her was Sparkle. Sparkle was crying and trying to fix her mascara. Mary felt sorry for her, but also knew that this was nothing out of the ordinary for the handbag sales associate. This was typical Sparkle! Ever since Mary had met Sparkle, she had known her to be, well, unstable and that was putting it mildly. Mary quickly waved and headed for the store.

There were three entrances to the HeidtMoore department store. The main entrance had the famed gold doors and sliding glass. The employee entrance that looked like a gateway to a prison, with dark, faintly lit hallways. This entrance led from the parking garage, to a single metal door with cracked paint, and a sign listing the vision of the HeidtMoore, a silhouette of Mr. Heidt fading into the background of the sign. The third entrance was the shipping and receiving dock, which also was the live animal entrance and housed about ten species of animal during any season. Mary had discovered this entry during her quick exit last spring when an active shooter appeared in the building. Since then she found the animal area somewhat comforting and occasionally brought snacks to the pets of the department store. Her favorite animals were the two penguins, that had recently been acquired from the London zoo. They were beautiful and Mary loved to feed them kippers.

Walking down the humid hallway of the employee entrance she caught up to T who was briskly walking ahead, obviously late for her shift.

"So, I nearly died this morning," Mary stated to T.

"Died? A bit dramatic Mer," T commented.

"Well I know 6 miles is nothing for you Ms. Marathon, but it was my first time and I literally thought I was going to die. My legs are like jelly," Mary replied. It was true, T ran marathons and thought nothing of doing ultramarathons for fun. Something Mary simply could not fathom.

"You'll get used to it. Where did he take you? Katy Trail again?"

"Yes, he looked so good. And I was a hot mess."

"Well you clean up well kid," T joked looking at Mary's hot pink suit. "It's like we planned it." Motioning to her hot pink puffed shoulder dress.

"Great minds think alike! Come on let's see what this day has for us! Do you think it will be Boggs or Sloan who texts us first this morning? Can you imagine if either of them were to replace Mr. Heidt?"

"Hi ladies!" Sloan said walking behind them and startling them.

"Oh hi! How are you?" said Mary, biting her lip.

"We are late for the meeting." Sloan said quickly moving past them. "After this morning's all store, T, will you make sure you have a coffee on my desk and fetch me some new ink cartridges for my printer, would you? Then grab the clothes for the meeting. Mary, I expect all your associates there." And with that, he was gone, out of view.

"Close call. You think he heard that?" Mary asked T nervously.

"No. He's far too preoccupied to even notice what we said. I'm surprised he even remembered my name."

As they walked through the employee entrance of the store, they noticed Olga standing at the end of the long, bleak hallway. She was talking very animatedly on her phone. Olga was one of the top salespeople at the HeidtMoore and the only associate who spoke Russian. She had a handful of international clients who shopped with her exclusively.

"Oblinsky, I have the money." She said, while vaping on a vape pen. "Yes. Yes. Tell Natalia the mink coat is here. See you at 3."

That was all Mary could hear and understand. Waving as they passed, Olga nodded and tossed her vape pen into her purse, then disappeared through the swinging doors into the Beauty department.

"That woman is crazy!" T whispered to Mary.

"I can never understand her."

"She has a big appointment today with her "special" Russian client," T said, while making the invisible quote signs with her hands. Mary knew what she meant.

There was a lot of drama last season due to an expensive emerald necklace going missing and Olga's Russian mafia clientele. The HeidtMoore was known for extravagant mannequin displays with runway outfits and coordinated high end jewelry and accessories to match. Nacho had told Mary over the summer about the case of the emerald necklace. A housekeeper had knocked over a mannequin while lip syncing one evening. It had fallen through one of the many holes in the floor and just by happenstance had landed practically in Olga's hands.

Unbeknownst to anyone, Olga's client had her eye on the piece, but never paid full price. So, Olga took it upon herself to stash the necklace for a bit, knowing full well that eventually it would go on sale. Nacho's team of investigators found the necklace she had stashed. There it lay, in a large hole in the wall in the back hallway of the Fine Five floor. Not only was the necklace in there but other accessories like Hermes belts, Versace scarves, a Chanel lapel pin, and three pairs of Gucci shoes. As it was an internal investigation no one really talked about the incident. All of the items were returned to the proper departments and security cameras were installed in all of the back hallways. Olga was given a slap on the wrist and no further criminal charges were pressed. Nacho did tell Mary, as a confidant, that the cameras were not actually connected or working due to budget constraints. They were merely for show.

"Is that okay for lunch?" T elbowed Mary snapping her out of her memory.

"Is what okay? Sorry, I was thinking about "Case of the Emerald Necklace," Mary replied.

"Oh, shh, don't talk about that out loud," T reminded Mary as they parted ways. "See you in a few at the meeting."

Even though a cold front was passing through, the temperatures the past few weeks had hovered near 100 degrees and it was by no means close to winter. But that didn't stop Sloan Garrett from conducting morning meetings about Fall designer arrivals nearly every day. Despite that most of the customers were still out of town, for him it was all about Fall. It was time to gear up and get the associates focused.

MORNING MEETING EVERYBODY IN THE FINE FIVE. TEN MINUTES. COMPLIMENTARY COFFEE AND DOUGHNUTS.

Sloan's voice echoed over the store microphone an hour before store opening.

CHOP CHOP EVERYONE! THIS IS A FALL PREVIEW DON'T BE LATE!

A few associates straggled in, onto the selling floor, including Rebecca, a selling associate who worked in Precious Jewelry. She made a bee line towards the table with doughnuts. She was followed by Zane, a beauty selling associate.

"This is the best thing about these dumb meetings" Rebecca said, stuffing a glazed doughnut into her mouth. "Want one?" She asked Zane.

"Oh Lord, no. I'm on a diet."

"Diet? You? You weigh about as much as a bird. Alright, I'll eat yours then." It was true. Zane had a tiny frame and was incredibly slim.

As soon as the assembled group of store associates were in the department, Sloan with microphone in hand, started the meeting.

"It's that time of year. Welcome to the fall preview!!!!" He said with great flourish, a la Hugh Jackman in 'The Greatest Showman'.

T, red faced and struggling to push the merchandise on to the floor, rolled out two racks of clothes. One rack was filled with expensive furs: minks, sables, and chinchillas. The second rack was filled with burgundy, mauve and jewel toned clothes in silks, satins, and velvet.

"Who's excited?" He asked the crowd of assembled associates, who were mostly milling around the coffee and doughnuts. No one responded.

"Is he crazy? Does he know it's August and also the hottest day of the year?" Rebecca asked Zane, hovering over the plate of freshly baked doughnuts.

"Yeah, there's no way I can sell any of that clothing. Are you kidding me? No one wants a mink and a burgundy sweater dress right now."

Sloan continued his meeting unaware that the majority of associates couldn't be less interested and had only come to the meeting for the free coffee and doughnuts.

"I have these fabulous furs. T, why don't you model one for us?"

T did as she was asked and put on a sable coat, perspiration dripping off her forehead.

"Isn't that gorgeous! How many of you can sell a mink or a sable today? Raise your hand." Not a hand was raised.

"On come on! You each have a customer. What if I offer you $50 in HeidtMoore rewards for selling a coat?" Suddenly three or four hands were raised.

"That's more like it. What about...$100 a coat?" A few more hands were raised. And that's how the selling incentives worked. Before the store opened that morning, Sloan was able to get each of the fifty or so associates to start thinking and planning for the upcoming fall season.

Relieved to be seated back at her desk after the meeting, T remembered the coffee for Sloan. She did as she was told and made Sloan his cappuccino. Then she went back downstairs for his ink cartridges and to pick up the daily mail. She scanned through a handful of letters in her hand.

"EVICTION, 3ʳᵈ WARNING, MUST PAY"

T instinctively knew that this was not good. This was more than your average junk mail.

"Sloan, what's this?" She asked once she got back upstairs.

He looked surprised when T handed him the mail.

"Weird. Don't worry about it." And he threw the mail in the trash. "Okay, grab a pen and paper. We've got business to do."

T's instinct was right. Working for Sloan, in his role as pseudo General Manager was going to be a nightmare. She longed for the old days with Mr. Heidt. He always treated her with respect and was never too needy. She certainly never had to make him his coffee.

SPARKLE

"Do you have a minute?" Sparkle asked, looking exceedingly guilty.

"Do I have a choice?" Tevi, Sparkle's manager, was very impatient as this was her last day before her two month-long trip away. Leaving the store would be bliss, but she had a lot to do before then. It did not include dealing with Sparkle, but as usual there was always something. Typical.

"Yes, Sparkle, what is it?" Tevi stared at the groveling associate before her.

"Can we go in the back?"

"To my office? Why can't you say what you need to say right here. Better yet, Chloe from the buying office should be here later, maybe she can help you?"

But Sparkle was already on her way towards the back of the sales floor. "Alright, have it your way. Let's go," Tevi said, giving in to her associate.

They left the Fendi handbag case line and walked towards Tevi's nondescript office, tucked away behind Gucci. It was no bigger than a broom closet.

"Make it quick. We don't have all day and I have a plane to catch."
Tevi never minced words.

"I am-" Sparkle froze.

"You are what? Go on, spit it out."

After a moment Sparkle spat out "I am pregnant."

Tevi burst out laughing, not believing her ears.

"You?" said Tevi incredulously. "With who's baby?! Wait." Suddenly
it dawned on Tevi that this could actually be a possibility and she became
serious. "Not Gottrocks!!!"

Thanks to Sparkle's shenanigans during the spring season, she had
almost single handedly destroyed a hugely important relationship
between the store and one of its top clients. It all happened when Sparkle
had forced herself upon the clients' son, Mr. Gottrocks Jr. It was more
than Tevi could handle and she wondered if she wasn't still traumatized
by the incident. But now this! Sparkle pregnant with his child!

"I'm not positive it's his."

"Not positive it's his? Good God, girl!" Tevi was in absolute disbelief,
her thick Anglo-Indian accent becoming pronounced.

Sparkle started crying again. "I know, it's awful. It's been three
months and now that I'm starting to show, I figured I better tell you."

"Who else's would it damn well be?" Now Tevi was becoming angry.

"No one. Well, I did go out with Chef once."

"You did what?" Tevi had to go. She didn't have the time for this
bullshit. "I told you not to go near that creep. Dear God. I have to go.
You had better sort yourself out girl."

On the way out the door, Tevi texted Brandi.

WE HAVE AN ISSUE! SPARKLE IS -

Then inserted a pregnant woman emoji and hit send. Just as Tevi was
rushing to get out of the department she passed Chef, who was carrying
a tray of delicious smelling fudge brownies.

"Whatsup' Tev? You want a sweet breakfast?" Chef was always borderline inappropriate with the female members of the staff, particularly Tevi. He licked his lips making her grimace. Being head chef of the HeidtMoore he assumed an all-powerful position, having clients fawn over him every day for his inexhaustible creative culinary talents.

"Who are those for? Someone special?", inquired Tevi, looking into Chef's pudgy perspiring face she couldn't tell who was worse; Gottrocks or the Chef.

As soon as Sparkle put the first brownie in her mouth, she couldn't stop. Crouched in the handbag stockroom, she proceeded to stuff her face.

"Baby, easy. Go easy on the brownies," said Chef with his arm around Sparkles waist.

"Yum, these are so good," she replied, crumbs spitting out of her mouth. At least she wasn't crying. "Can I ask you a question?"

"Anything you want babe." Chef was as slick as ever.

"It's only me that you're seeing, right? I mean, we're going to be together now, right?"

"We are together. We always have been," said Chef in a soothing voice.

Sparkle didn't know this was a complete lie. Chef had been carrying out an affair the season prior with the assistant head of Human Resources, Brandi. Both of their jobs were on the line, but Chef didn't care. He played by his own rules. He was head chef after all and could do as he pleased.

Brandi, the bubbly blond he'd been messing around with, would never find out about Sparkle. If she did, what would she do? Fire him? He had enough dirt on her to bring down the HeidtMoore empire. With her alcoholic escapades and hot and heavy trysts with employees in the stairwells of the department store. To be fair, it had only ever been with Chef, but no one else needed to know that.

In Chef's mind, Brandi would get what was coming to her, were she to find out. Had she been more attentive to him, like promoting him to

Top Chef de Cuisine, instead of simply "chef" and given him a raise and a gold name plate for his door, Chef might not have felt the need to look elsewhere for a bit of fun.

The truth was Brandi had hired Chef and she certainly could fire Chef but that thought didn't even cross his mind.

Chef kissed Sparkle on the forehead, then went to the seventh floor to the Pingüino restaurant to prep for the afternoon's service.

The Pingüino was the HeidtMoore's once acclaimed restaurant. Its interior, a chic black, white, and grey toned opulent dining hub away from the hustle and bustle of the store, was starting to show signs of neglect. Due to lack of funding, the restaurant had not been updated since the early eighties. Despite this the restaurant was still expected to sell over five million dollars annually. That's where the chef came in. He made his name as a celebrity chef who appeared on a weekly cooking show called, "Cooking with Chef."

In the spring season, Chef had prepared a luncheon for the Gottrocks, the store's top client. That led to Mr. Gottrocks Jr. securing Chef a contract with a network cable station. Unfortunately, his new fame meant his ego ballooned exponentially.

"Chef is a nightmare. He always thinks he's better than everyone else," associates would occasionally complain to Human Resources. Since Frank, the head of Human Resources, had retired at the beginning of the summer, Brandi, his assistant, had to hear all of the issues.

"That's it. I quit!" said one of the dishwashers one day, sitting in Brandi's office.

"Now, now. It isn't that bad. You can't quit anyway. It's not professional. You must at least give two weeks' notice."

"He is a beast!" Brandi knew only too well what a *beast* chef could be. "He shouts and screams, and he puts people down. Mi hermana, she works on the line and he says bad stuff behind her back. I can't do this anymore."

After an hour of listening to him voice his complaints and persuading him he didn't need to quit, it was time for Brandi to take a break. She took a sip from her pink Yeti flask, removed her flipflops, which had been hidden from view under the desk, and put on her hot pink stilettos to walk the store.

Starting on level six, Brandi walked down through each department stopping occasionally to talk to an associate. While she missed having Frank as a mentor, she enjoyed the freedom of not having to report to a boss. She was now the boss. It was everything she had ever wanted, and she wasn't yet thirty years old. Who else was lucky enough to get this sort of responsibility at such a young age? She was in charge of Human Resources for the largest department store in the world! But was she up to all of the extra work that would now be a part of the job? She wasn't entirely sure, if she was being honest with herself. But, as Scarlet O'Hara would say, "tomorrow is another day." She would think about it then. For now, she would do the part of her job she enjoyed the most: talking to associates and 'checking in' with them.

"How's it going Ginger?" Brandi asked an associate who was restocking a shelf with Hanky Panky panties in the Heaven or Hell intimates department.

"Fine. Thank you. Actually, er, my name is Greer."

"Oh, that's right! Duh." Feeling a sudden breeze coming from a vent in the ceiling. "Wow, it's really cold over here. Like Antarctica. How do you stand it?"

"That's why I'm wearing a sweater in August."

"Do you like it here? Working in this department?"

"Yes, I do. But I may need to talk to you later. It's about my health insurance," said the timid associate.

"Okay! Sure, no problem. Call me." Brandi said, making a phone motion with her hand and picking up a pair of underwear with the other. "Oh, and Ginger, would you put some of these on my house account?"

"Sure," said Greer slightly startled by the absolute lack of professionalism and interest in her concern.

Brandi had reached the third floor Men's department and was exiting the escalator before she realized she did not have her cell phone with her. *Damn it!* How people survived before the days of cell phones she did not know. As she retraced her footsteps getting back on the escalator, she saw Sparkle coming down in the opposite direction. Sparkle seemed unusually perky to Brandi this morning.

"Hi Brandi," Sparkle exclaimed a little too loudly upon seeing Brandi.

As they passed by each other, Brandi gave a slight smile and waved. "Good morning." There was something about that girl that Brandi didn't quite trust. But she couldn't put her finger on it.

"What's up with her?" Brandi said aloud. Zane just happened to be behind Brandi on the escalator.

"So…I heard she's preggers."

"What? Sparkle? Nooo." Brandi scoffed at the very idea.

"That's the word on the street. And look how she's walking." Zane then impersonated a pregnant woman walking. Brandi almost burst out laughing. "But who is the father?" Zane continued. "That's what I want to know." Zane winked at Brandi.

"It better not be true. That means she'll have to be on a leave of absence. Ugh. Nooo. We need her selling and not having a baby. We're in a hiring freeze right now and we need all the help we can get for the fall and spring seasons."

"Why on earth would someone do something like that? Get pregnant right before the holiday season? Like, duh. It's probably just a rumor anyway. But you know she had a thing with a customer AND apparently someone in the store. But who knows. Gotta' go. Tootles." Zane scuttled past her, disappearing into the handbag department.

While Brandi knew vaguely about the incident with Sparkle and the customer, she acted like she also knew all about the affair with the associate. She wracked her brain as to *who* it could possibly be. *Oh Lord. Another HR issue I'll have to deal with.* Thought Brandi.

MAPPING IT OUT

The HeidtMoore was a huge department store and to be a manager you had to be tough, resilient and a real go-getter. The store was over 100 million square feet encompassing six levels. It housed a giant aquarium in the center of the store, plus a small zoo of live animals in the basement that were used for their award-winning window displays. One needed athletic prowess to cover the store in a day. And to do it in 85mm Louboutin heels, as so many of the female managers did, was a real strength.

At the first-floor entrance was the world-renowned cosmetics department with over 200 counters of make-up, fragrances, and body enhancers to nip, tuck, and accentuate whatever you wanted. Also, on the first-floor guests could shop exclusive HeidtMoore food items in one of the largest gourmet food emporiums in the country.

The second floor housed a fabulous precious jewelry department. Every gemstone and diamond glistened brightly under the lights. If this weren't enough to capture the clients interest, the exotic designer handbags and magnificent array of ladies shoes would entice anyone to shop. There always seemed to be a bit more hustle and bustle with customers and associates alike on this particular floor of the HeidtMoore.

On the third floor, customers could shop the Men's World, a masculine hub for the gentleman. Then a short distance away was Heaven or Hell, otherwise known as the intimate apparel department. A department strategically placed close to men's.

Children's, Gift Galleries, Athleisure and Tech were all on the fourth floor. Shortly before Mary was hired, the Athleisure and Tech departments were added to this floor as they were new concepts for the emerging millennial customer. The Children's department rivaled Hamley's, the British multinational toy retailer. Gift Galleries was recently renamed Gifts & Home as a more comforting component for the retail experience. Its plush interiors of luxurious textiles showcased antiques and modern home décor. From a William IV armchair to a Jean-Michel Basquiat painting, there was something for everyone.

Couture was on the fifth floor. The top designers from around the world coveted their location on floor five, otherwise known as "the Fine Five." The far corner of this floor housed the Contemporary area for the aspiring Couture shopper. If the customer wanted to rest after a full day of shopping floors one through five, they could relax at the glamourous spa on the sixth floor. There was also the famous restaurant, The Pingüino. Although a little outdated it was still a place where all the influencers and bloggers went to see and be seen. It didn't hurt that the restaurant was run by a celebrity chef named Chef.

Most of the managers were Lifers. And all brought different skill sets to the role. For example, Tevi and Sarafina. Both had the qualities needed to manage at the HeidtMoore: tenacity, strength of mind and business acumen. Both managers, however, had vastly different management styles. Tevi managed the Handbags and Cosmetics departments. This was no easy job being responsible for departments located on different floors.

Tevi was more of a dictator and not one of her associates was ever seen just standing around the sales floor. They had to be working, selling as much as possible. Tevi would frequently demand they come to her office "immediately" and explain to her in detail how many customers they had contacted, how much they had sold for the day and what their game plan was to sell more. If the associate failed to provide the information Tevi was looking for, she would get HR involved. If they gave her the information she was looking for, they would be released back to the selling floor. Since the disappearance and apparent suicide of Mr. Heidt, selling and overachieving goals was never more vital for the managers if they wanted to move up the ranks of the HeidtMoore.

Then there was Sarafina. Sarafina ran the biggest volume driver in the HeidtMoore, yet her associates never seemed engaged, or even cared to leave the large, carpeted area which marked the perimeter of the precious jewelry counters. It was bewildering to other managers. She was kind, generous to a fault, mild mannered and she always wore couture.

"You look amazing. Who are you wearing?" One might say.

"Valentino. Fall '14"

"Wow. I love!"

"What size are you? This dress should fit you. Hardly ever been worn. You can have it. I don't really want it anymore."

A week later, the associate would receive the dress in a HeidtMoore tote, having been dry cleaned, ready for its next owner.

Being a "Lifer" Sarafina knew to speak fluent retail jargon. Her discussions of business were always filled with acronyms such as, "TY" for "this year" and "LY" for "last year." It took Mary nearly 4 months to figure out what she was talking about most of the time. Now, Mary found herself communicating with the other managers the same way.

"TY by EOM, we need the comp numbers up 4% to plan or Sloan will schedule a PK every day!"

Mary was fortunate she had made friends with both Tevi and Sarafina during her first months at the HeidtMoore. She and Tevi bonded one day over pears, of all things. It seemed that the pear was some fruit they both enjoyed and happened to both have for lunch on the same day! Before bonding over a pear, Tevi had always seemed a bit intense to her, a person she would not want to piss off. Tevi was from India and had studied in England. Every sentence began with "bloody this" or "bloody that." Mary had heard terrible stories of how mean Tevi could be to other co-workers. Mary was not one for confrontation and wanted very much to stay on Tevi's good side, so she was thrilled when all it took was a pear to make a new friend.

It was tradition at the HeidtMoore that managers ate lunch with other managers. That golden hour of the day when you could vent out frustrations, gossip, and count down the remaining hours, minutes, seconds of the day.

T had asked Mary to lunch the first week she started working at the HeidtMoore which is how she found out so much about the inner workings of the massive department store. Mary found it quite a blessing that she had the afternoon meal with different managers each day. On the second week of working at the HeidtMoore she had had lunch with Tevi, Hilz and Sarafina. She felt kind of, 'popular', for one shining moment. Instinctually Mary knew that it was in her best interest to befriend the managers, and to be a good manager herself. She needed the respect of the associates who would be working for her.

The morning had passed, and it was time for the routine *"what's for lunch"* conversations. Mary went down to the Handbag department to find Tevi and to see what her plans were for the afternoon meal. The choices for lunch were few: bring something from home and eat free, eat upstairs at Pingüino, and pay a lot for fine dining, or walk down to Flirty Birds and pay some for a mediocre meal. Mary usually rotated between the choices depending on whom she was eating with.

She found Tevi on the sales floor with a customer who appeared to be finishing up her handbag purchase.

"Thank you, Mrs. Crawley, for your patience. The bag took a few days longer than expected to get here, but you can see it was worth the wait!" This would be her last sale before her vacation.

Tevi proceeded to uncover a large stingray tote bag by IHAYD. The IHAYD handbags, a relatively new brand to the HeidtMoore, had gained huge popularity amongst celebrities in the past year. An acronym for: I Have and You Don't, the personalized bags each came with a lavish hangtag swinging from the handles of each one of the ten styles the handbag came in. The department had been surpassing sales plans as a result of these bags and Tevi was relishing every minute of her success. Boggs was thrilled too since it was his idea to try them in the first place.

Tevi finished her conversation with Mrs. Crawley, completed wrapping up her new purchase and then showed the customer out the door. She waited until the customer had reclaimed her car – a Bentley – at the valet and was driving away before she ran back to the counter.

"That bloody Crawley loves those damn bags! Always wants to spend my time trying to decide if she *needs* it knowing bloody well that she doesn't. C'mon let's get off this floor," Tevi groaned, as she led the way back to her office.

Mary following behind her said, "Well it looks like your day is more productive than mine has been. Let's go eat."

"Oh no, I haven't had a minute. I don't have time for lunch. My taxi is already here. Has been for the last thirty bloody minutes. Oh, by the way, Sparkle dropped a goddamn bloody bomb on me first thing this morning. I will text you when I get to the airport and fill you in. Tell T I will call her shortly."

"That's right, I forgot, you are leaving today! Don't you run into famous people every year out there? Who do you think you will run into this year?"

"God only knows. Last year I saw Salma Hayek. Couldn't have been nicer. Lovely woman." Then, back in her office, she grabbed her Louis Vuitton roller and her Loewe tote and headed back out the door. "Bye!" She said to Mary and blew air kisses. With that, Tevi was through the gold doors of the HeidtMoore and in a limo en route to the airport.

Mary wandered up to the Pingüino for an overpriced fish taco. She hoped the afternoon would be busier than the morning had been. Upstairs, at the exclusive restaurant, Mary was seated in the corner, at the very back of the restaurant. 'Siberia' is what this particular area of the restaurant was called because it was so far back and none of the customers ever wanted to be seated there. Mary didn't mind. She liked it, except for the draft that came through one of the vents that hung overhead.

"Excuse me," Mary called out to one of the waitresses, named Roxy.

"Yes, what can I do for you today madam?" said the overly polite waitress.

"You don't need to call me madam, really. I was wondering, though, if you wouldn't mind turning down the vent. It's a bit chilly." Mary said, teeth chattering.

Then with a sudden change of tone, Roxy, a heavy-set woman in her late fifties with died purple hair and purple eye shadow, gave Mary a peculiar look.

"Whatever you want Mary." She sighed heavily at the request. "And did you decide on what you want to eat?"

"The norm. Just the tacos." Mary said lightheartedly.

"We're out. What else?" Roxy answered back hastily.

"I'll do the cheeseburger then."

"Not exactly a slim down meal Mary." *Yikes! What was Roxy implying?* Mary felt slightly paranoid all of a sudden. She also hoped Roxy wasn't saying things like this to the customers. It certainly wouldn't help the store's reputation. "Looks like what's-her-face over there has had a few too many cheeseburgers," Roxy stated raising her eyebrows. She grabbed the menu from Mary and stormed off.

What did that mean? Mary was quickly losing her appetite. She looked over and caught a glimpse of Sparkle coming out of the kitchen. *That was strange. She should be on the floor, selling things.* The very moment Sparkle caught Mary's eye, she quickly turned away and tried to move as fast as she could out of the restaurant, but not before Chef came out and had a few words with her. Mary watched them like a hawk. Something wasn't quite right about the pair of them.

Moments later, Mary's cheeseburger arrived. Her appetite was restored.

Roxy came back to check on Mary. "Everything is great, thank you Roxy."

"Good, I'm glad. I'd say I'll send your compliments to the Chef, but he rarely cooks anymore. Between us," Roxy looked around conspiratorially, "he won't last long the rate he's going. You mark my words."

After only finishing half her meal, Mary paid with her HeidtMoore reward money and was almost glad to go back to work.

MARY'S PROMOTION

It was important to Mary to always be on time for work. Whether first thing in the morning or getting back from lunch on time, she was an absolute stickler for punctuality. She assumed this was why she had just been promoted to manage all of the areas on the fourth floor of the HeidtMoore so quickly. The executives knew that with Mary, they had someone they could rely on.

When she started at the HeidtMoore, she was managing the Children's department. That was eight months ago. Within three months, she was asked to oversee the Gifts & Home department on the same floor. The previous manager, Kathy, had a nervous breakdown and had to leave. And now, Mary had been promoted yet again. This time it was to manage the Athleisure and Tech department. However, with all the promotions, Mary wasn't seeing an increase in her salary. This was problematic. It was a topic of conversation she needed to have with Brandi, who was harder and harder to meet with these days. Mary's numerous emails to her proved futile.

It was these four departments: Gifts & Home, Children's, Athleisure, and Tech, that made up the fourth floor of the famous HeidtMoore department store that Mary now managed. The revered department store had a total of 6 stories in all. It was the most famous department store in the world, opened in the early 1940's by Mr. Herbert Heidt and his long-time friend Mr. Abraham Moore. They purchased the building and transformed it into a lavish department store with limestone bricks and 24-carat gold doors. Every floor was made of gold-dusted marble and the walls housed different departments all centered around the largest indoor aquarium in the country. To reach the floors, customers traveled on the custom-built spiraling escalator surrounding the aquarium, providing a magnificent view of each floor below.

When Heidt Sr. held the reins to the store, it was always immaculate with yearly paint touch-ups, boutique renovations, etc. When he handed the store over to his son it was at first, a smooth transition. In fact, the current Mr. Heidt spared no expense on fashion events and on hosting noted designers. However, that all changed with the introduction of the world wide web. The HeidtMoore had struggled to keep up with the ever-changing technology. Mr. Heidt and his Board of Directors pushed with much capital outlay to boost the stores website. With this focus, the store seemed to freeze in time and seemed neglected and a bit irrelevant.

Some areas of the store where customers shopped were getting shabby and in great need of renovation. The grim environment of the stockrooms and managers offices was worthy of note. In most cases, these rooms served a dual purpose. This was less than ideal, especially with regard to the managers having confidential conversations with their associates.

Mary walked into her grim, chain link bordered office, and threw down her handbag. She quickly pulled up the Spark board for daily sales numbers.

Spark was the internal electronic system used by executives and managers to look at sales numbers. It was an excellent and easy resource unless, of course the computers were down – which happened frequently. Then everyone was in trouble. It was not Mary's favorite part of the job, but it was an important one. Especially since the fall season was beginning. This was the busiest time of year for retail, and HeidtMoore was no exception. Mary planned on being as organized as possible. Looking at her watch she recognized she was late.

"Damn! Not again." She quickly left the office, locking the chain link door behind her and headed to the executive office.

She arrived just in the nick of time. Every morning all the managers huddled together in the executive offices for a startup meeting. They had to review the previous day's business and the plan for the current day. It was only supposed to be a short 15-minute meeting, but usually ended up finishing 30 minutes late. Fortunately, Spark was working properly today. It was always a gamble as to whether the software would be working. As with most things at the HeidtMoore, it was way past time for an upgrade to the system, as well.

Mary jotted down the numbers ol' school style, as in a pen and post-it, and taped it to her phone. She glanced at her Apple watch again to read an incoming message.

Enjoyed the run yesterday. Did you make it here on time today?

The message from Nacho made her smile. She picked up her phone and texted back immediately.

Yep, tea latte too….

Then the pause. She wanted to type *XOXO* or *Love* but hesitated. Instead Mary inserted running emoji 🏃 . Her finger wavered over the heart emoji, but she settled on a smiley face 😊 . Grabbing her latte, Mary headed to the executive office.

Already assembled in the executive office were a few other managers and Sloan. As an Assistant General Manager, or AGM's as they were referred to, he was known for micromanaging all his teams and was often rude to anyone from whom he needed nothing. However, in the last couple of months, he was lightening up a bit and seemed a little more sincere. Many wondered if he had found a love interest outside of work. There had to be some reason for this change in personality.

The other AGM was Boggs Daniel. He was an ex-cheerleader who always found a silver lining, but never knew when to draw the line, especially in matters pertaining to business. For example, last season when he saw Bella Hadid on the front page of Women's Wear Daily wearing moonboots, he proceeded to order an unprecedented number without any research into buying trends.

Boggs was Sloan's nemesis and like him, Boggs was striving to be the next General Manager of the HeidtMoore. The one goal they currently had in common was their desire to have the HeidtMoore succeed this fall, especially with the drama surrounding Mr. Heidt, who had been out of the store for nearly a year. Mary felt sad that she would never get to meet the Man in Charge now that he was allegedly dead. Too bad.

Sloan, looked up from his papers, removed his gold rimmed Warby Parker, readers and began slightly bouncing on his toes.

"Okay, we have another minute or so. T, who are we waiting on?"

T, the executive assistant for the HeidtMoore, looked up from her computer.

"Not sure, did you look at the schedule?" She slid the paper with the schedule over to him. Sloan picked up the sheet and reviewed quickly.

"Okay, Leigha, here, Nacho, here, Sarafina, here, Mary, here, Sam," looking around the room. "Sam, okay not here yet Hilz?" Glancing down to look at the schedule again. "Okay so Sam and Hilz are probably on their way, let's get started." He tossed the schedule to the side and addressed the few managers who had assembled for the morning meeting.

"First, a note from Boggs. He will be back tomorrow but insisted that I share the email this morning. We want to congratulate Mary once again on her promotion to running the entire fourth floor," Sloan said, putting extra emphasis on the word "entire." "This is quite an achievement for someone so new to the HeidtMoore."

Mary thought that was nice of Boggs to remember, but it always made her uncomfortable being called out in front of her peers. Sending an email was even more embarrassing! Mary put a lot of pressure on herself to succeed, and the more people paid attention to her the more pressure she felt.

As Sloan was continuing with other announcements, Sam and Hilz tiptoed into the office hoping no one would notice their tardiness.

Sam was the Fine Five manager, a gay man in his mid-fifties who most employees referred to as a Lifer.

A *Lifer* was someone who had worked at the HeidtMoore for over 15 years, and this had basically been their only job, ever. Sarafina and Leigha

38

were also Lifers. There were dozens at the HeidtMoore, and they were the ones who always started or ended conversations with, *"Heidt Senior would be rolling in his grave!"* Hilz had joined the store shortly after Mary to run the Contemporary department, which housed thousands of labels, appealing mostly to the sixteen to thirty-five-year-old demographic. Not new to the company, Hilz had spent years in the buying office, and never let anyone forget it. She was in her late thirties, loud and overweight, but Mary thought she was a retail genius and really very funny. The way she managed her employees, all thirty of them, amazed Mary. Mary wanted the confidence and retail smarts that Hilz brought to the business. Hilz gave the impression that she had probably never had a sweaty palm in her life, or so Mary thought.

Sloan saw the two in the corner of the office, "Okay why don't the two tardy members of the meeting start with your numbers." Referring to Sam and Hilz. *Damn. They had been noticed.* Hilz of course spoke up, much to the relief of Sam, who tended to stutter when put on the spot.

"We made the sales plan yesterday and are beating last year by 40%. I just got off the phone with Hayley Moore at the buying office and we have the entire fall calendar jam packed with meetings and events."

Knowing that whenever Hilz got the floor to speak, it could take an entire thirty minutes for her to finish, it was time for Sloan to interrupt.

"Thank you Hilz" he said, interrupting, "I will get with Hayley on the calendar event. What do you need for today to make plan?"

Hilz, answering bubbly, "Oh, just 250 thousand. We will do it." Sloan, looked at Sam.

"Thank you. Sam, what about the Fine Five? How much business do you need to do today?"

As the rest of the managers continued explaining their sales plans, Mary's eyes wandered over to Nacho. She did her best to refrain from making eye contact with him during meetings, but it never failed that it happened at least once. The two had been seeing each other for four months now, but only a couple of people at work knew how serious their relationship was. Over the summer some of the managers would hang out after work at their local work bar, Flirty Birds, and this is where Mary and Nacho became more than just friends.

Mary also made friends with T over the spring and summer months and had several "girls' nights out" with her as work became more and more stressful. Mary was finding out quickly one way to succeed in the wild world of retail was to have close friends in the same world. T was one of them.

"Mary. Mary… hello Mary?" Sloan was trying to catch her attention. Mary, deep in thought about Nacho's clinging t-shirt from the morning run the day before, caused her to blush. Her hands sweaty, barely griping the latte in one hand and turning her phone over with the other to read her numbers. Every morning she posted sticky notes to the back of her phone with all of the daily sales numbers from the day before. It took her a moment to gain her composure.

Sloan snapped his fingers, trying to get Mary's attention. Mary glanced up only to see Sloan rolling his eyes. *Unbelievable. He's so impatient.* But she wouldn't let him get the better of her and allow him to belittle her in front of her colleagues. No, she would show him just how competent she was and how she could drive sales for the HeidtMoore.

"Oh yes, well Tech had a great day yesterday, so did Children's. 60k in each division. But Gifts and the Athleisure departments struggled a little. Hopefully today will be good, we need 25, 50, 45, and 15 dollars," she said chuckling, "kidding that's thousands of course."

"Thank you, Mary. Yes, you do need to make up those numbers." It bothered Mary that he never congratulated her victories, but only seemed to criticize the things that weren't working, like trying to overachieve impossible goals in some of the store's most difficult departments, like Gifts & Home. That department just wasn't selling anymore. Not like it used to. It was once a leading department, but now the HeidtMoore customer was making gift purchases online. The traffic in the department was at an all-time low and it didn't help that most the associates in the department were ancient. At least half of the associates who worked in Gifts & Home were over the age of seventy and they all remembered the glory days of the department store. Mary really struggled getting them to conform to the new way that the HeidtMoore was being run, much less getting them to use an iPhone with all of the app features.

Sloan continued with his meeting agenda. "Well, Boggs gets back from his week-long vacation tomorrow, so I'm it for today and I'll be walking the floors. Text me if you need me, but no group texts! Got it? I don't need everyone texting with emojis or whatever they're called." Despite the advances in technology at the HeidtMoore, Sloan was not very advanced in certain areas. "Make it an opulent day everyone."

At that very moment, in unison, everyone exited and put their heads down to their phones. Very robotic.

And that was how every day at the HeidtMoore started.

T'S AFTERNOON

"Have a wonderful time, and yes your calls will be forwarded to Sloan, don't worry and relax." T hung up the phone with Tevi, slightly jealous. She would give anything to have a 60-day hiatus from the store.

T and Tevi had worked together for at least six years and Tevi was one of the few managers T really trusted, Mary being another. Tevi was efficient, did her job and could, on occasion, be a bitch. That didn't bother T so much. If anything, she admired Tevi for being so forthright. And besides, Tevi sold. Lots. Without Tevi, the store always felt like it was coming apart. Never a good feeling. They got along well and often mused about the state of the HeidtMoore and what the future had in store.

"Do you know, sometimes I feel like a musician on the Titanic, working at the HeidtMoore." T mused. "Just playing along, until the bitter end."

"And who am I? Bloody Kate Winslet? I'd like to find myself a Leonardo DiCaprio, that's for sure."

Tevi didn't let the state of the business get her down, unlike T. She just charged on and did her work.

Something else that was getting T down was the amount of work she had to do. It seemed the worse off the company was, the more work was piled on T's plate. Most of which she didn't even sign up for, and truthfully, she felt it was just dumped on her because no one else would take the time. At first, T thought taking on more initiatives throughout the store was a great way to get ahead and move into another role. It wasn't long before she realized she was being taken advantage of. Currently she was working to develop an associate contest to motivate associates to sell more. It stressed her out because it was a task Boggs had so abruptly given her. She instantly recalled her last conversation with him before his vacation.

"Come on T, we have another amazing project for you. This time it has to do with creating a contest. You're gonna' put the contest on a TV screen in the employee hallway for everyone to look at when they arrive to the store for their shift."

"But Boggs, first of all, what TV screen?"

"We need to put up TV screens downstairs, part of our 'Go Digital' initiative." Boggs said, seemingly unfazed by making the request.

"But I have no experience with creating contests and putting them on TV screens. How do I even do that?"

"Figure it out. I gotta go." Boggs said, packing some files into his bricfcase and finishing off what was left of half a salami sandwich.

"Okay." T took a deep breath. "When does this need to be done?"

"I want it done by the time I'm back."

"What?!"

"If you need to send a clip of what you've done to me while I'm out that's fine. This contest is huge. Make it big." Then Boggs left, leaving T with a project she had no idea how to begin or how to produce.

Before so much work had been left on T's lap, she had volunteered to participate in several important initiatives for the company. There were the expected tasks, like organizing the store holiday party and Dallas community volunteer efforts. This was a good way to move up in the company – or so she thought. Then there were new committees such as, heading up the Instagram accounts, creating live stream videos for store events – which she soon figured out how to do as she designed her first interactive video contest, making commercial-like movies promoting new products, and leading the in-store tech teams – whatever that might mean. The last initiative was very perplexing, as no one had told her what exactly she was meant to be doing with the 'tech teams'. Who were the tech teams? What was the tech? And how could they even run the teams with new technology when the store had no money? It was all very daunting.

The one thing T did know was that she was responsible for issuing all company phones to the store selling associates. It must have been a job no one else wanted to do and so it was passed on to T, who accepted it demonstrating a gesture of goodwill. Sadly the "goodwill" was turning into hostility. The associates were demanding. Not only that, but some of them also barely knew where the email function was, let alone how to post on Instagram. It was turning into a nightmare and driving T to drink. Now, she was finding herself stopping more frequently at Trader Joe's for the famous "Two Buck Chuck" bottles of wine. If one thing were true, it was that T could not let herself turn into Brandi. It may have been one of the store's best kept secrets, that the HeidtMoore's assistant Human Resources Manager was a full-blown alcoholic. Now, at least, T had empathy.

"Hey, Sista'. Is my phone ready?" said Ta'Keisha, ten minutes after handing the iPhone to T.

Ta'Keisha worked in Men's fragrances and was one of the last associates to get an iPhone.

"Not yet Ta'Keisha. Still working on it." T said, fiddling around with the phone. "I just don't understand how you were able to delete your selling app? It's the one thing you really need to be able to…sell. It's also an un-removable function on all of our iPhones." T was thoroughly confused as to how she could have done this. As was Ta'Keisha.

"It's a what?"

"It's something that is impossible to remove from the phone."

"Sista' girl! I don't need no iPhone to run my business." Was her response to the company issued phone. T knew it would be an uphill struggle getting her on board. At least, she had the phone and was willing to have it set up.

T, sitting at a desk, surrounded by twenty phones, tried to respond calmly. It wasn't easy and she bit her lip to keep her cool and collected.

"Oh no. Wait. Where is your?" T said, trailing off.

"My what?"

"What exactly did you do? There isn't an email icon."

"What's that?"

T questioned whether or not this was a serious question. After a moment, she took out her own phone to show her.

"It's an icon like this." pointing her to the @ icon. "You see this box? This is called an icon, you have many of them, and when you press it, it takes you to the internet."

"That's cool! But how do I email my client?"

It was going to be an exceedingly long afternoon for T.

After an hour of walking through the many apps, making sure the email was properly set up and uploading contacts for Ta'Keisha, T was ready for a break.

Just as T was leaving, Sloan shot through the door.

"T! Help me get on a call with Mrs. Ivory."

"Sure, I'm just leaving for a break, but..."

"T! This is urgent."

"Of course, I'll do that right now for you." T knew she would never get a break and she had been working on iPhones nonstop for the last five hours.

"So, I want to show Mrs. Ivory these pictures on the phone. But how do I do it?" Sloan had opened up his gallery and was showing some of the worst pictures T had ever seen. *Was he kidding?*

"You want to show Mrs. Ivory these pictures?" The pictures were taken by Sloan of various merchandise throughout the store. The problem was they were all either out of focus or the products were only halfway in the frame. Plus, you couldn't tell *what* the product was and didn't photograph well, or all of the above.

This was a disaster.

"You are sending these out? You can't do that Sloan."

"What do ya' mean, I can't do that? Sure, I can. Okay, well, maybe not that one." He said scrolling over to one of the photos that was just a blur.

"None of them. Let me help you. I'll go down to the floor and take a few shots, ok?"

"Sure. You think you know how to sell from photos, be my guest, T, and snap away. Just know she's looking at shoes, jewelry and some gift ideas."

T could tell his ego was a little bruised, but better that, than send out less than clear photos to the HeidtMoore's top client.

Thirty minutes later, T was back.

She had captured an assortment of items which were, to T, the best of the best of what the HeidtMoore had to offer. She entered Sloan's office, ignoring the ten associates who had congregated outside to see her.

"Let's see what you think of these."

T showed Sloan a beautiful pair of Manolo Blahnik shoes with several different color options; pink, tiger print, white and yellow, several Jay Strongwater pieces, Stephen Webb necklaces, as well as a handful of other items that might work well as gifts. Sloan was impressed.

"Nice photo skills T!"

"Thanks, you just need to make sure what you want to show Mrs. Ivory is something she can *actually see*. Not something blurry, otherwise you'll never make a sale."

Two hours later Sloan thanked T for making a twenty-thousand-dollar sale. Ironically, T made no commission from this despite her helping find the product and take the pictures.

The next thing T knew, she was teaching a photo technique and sharing class for which Sloan had volunteered her. He even went on to Amazon and purchased a new iPad, tripod, and camera! All of which T would barely put to use. Oh well, it was the thought that counted, but what about the store budget? It seemed to T that the more the store was in debt, the more they kept spending.

Something wasn't adding up...

T texted Mary.

OMG. Sloan just purchased $4000 worth of crap for me to teach these classes and I have no idea what I'm doing LOL 😀

Moments later Mary responded.

That's BS. No offense. The store can't afford to fix the holes in the floors or upgrade the 1980's wallpaper in the fitting rooms. Wtf?

The very next day, T inspected the giant Amazon box that had just arrived in the executive office. She unwrapped the box and took out the tripod, for what purpose she would need this, she had no idea. An Apple laptop, a speaker, the latest iPhone X, and a complimentary $5 shopping coupon were also in the box.

"Great, it arrived! Your first class is tomorrow at 9 a.m. Excited?" said Sloan coming into the office.

"I can't believe you ordered this!"

"I know, right? How cool!"

"No, I meant...I don't even know how or what to do with this." T was panicking inside. Teach a class on what? She had to teach herself how to use the tripod for starters.

"It'll be a breeze. Don't worry." Sloan was always so reassuring.

The remainder of the day was spent googling how to install the speakers, what programs to use, and watching YouTube tutorials.

Brring BRRing.

Damnit. T pressed pause on the how-to video on her phone and walked over to the landline that was on her desk.

"Good afternoon. Thank you for calling the HeidtMoore. This is T in the executive Office. How may I help you?"

"Your company is a fraud!!!!" yelled the voice on the other end of the line.

"I'm sorry?" said T, slightly taken aback.

"I've had $2000 worth of merchandise charged to my card and I did not spend that much money I assure you and I am about to report you to the local news station. I want the whole world to know what a fraud the HeidtMoore is."

"I'm sorry, who am I talking to?" This was unbelievable. Today of all days. "I didn't catch your name."

"Charlene Prickle."

BOGGS PERU

Boggs returned home from his week vacation in the wine country to his sleek mid-century modern home in Highland Park. Various shades of white covered the walls and furniture fabrics. The accents were faux fur, and an occasional Jan Barboglio piece was placed here and there. The house had 4 bedrooms and was really far too large for just him and Rod.

He couldn't wait to pour himself a glass of wine from one of his newly purchased bottles of Pinot Grigio and then FaceTime Rod.

Rod had been Boggs' partner for over twenty years. He was currently on a mission trip to Peru. Yet again, Rod had taken on a new venture that paid little, if anything. Although in the past Boggs wished that Rod had a project that paid something so he wouldn't always have to be the bread winner, the timing was actually particularly good this time. They had been having serious issues and the communication was not good between them. There was also the matter of Rod's weight gain, which stressed Boggs to no end. He even went so far as to purchase a ticket for Rod to tour Machu Pichu, a subtle hint that walking the ancient ruins would be good for him.

But the conversation leading up to Rod's exotic trip was all but smooth...

"I'm going to be teaching English to poor children in shanty towns. I don't have time to go sightseeing," said Rod shortly before his trip to South America.

"It isn't sightseeing, you get to exercise." Boggs could not have cared less about the historical significance of the ancient ruins.

"What are you saying? You don't think I'm fit enough?" Rod was hurt by this implication.

"No, no that's not what I'm saying. I just think you need to continue taking long walks and doing more active things."

"Nothing is more active than teaching poor kids the alphabet Boggs. What are *you* doing to help others?"

There it was a blow to the ego.

There was no more discussion on the matter. Instead Boggs gathered up his briefcase and coat and went to work.

The following week Rod was on a flight to Peru.

After getting the wine from the cellar, Boggs sat down on the plush sofa. He stared at his Apple laptop, a little hesitant to lift the screen and to start dialing. He loosened his collar, took a sip from his Baccarat glass filled with vintage wine, and proceeded to FaceTime Rod.

Boggs entered his password. A box popped up.

Incorrect password. Try again.

He couldn't believe his password wasn't working. It was the same one he had been using for the past ten years. He tried again. Still nothing. He tried several different combinations before resigning himself to calling the help desk. This was the last thing he wanted to do.

"Hello? Hello? Can you hear me? I need a password reset!" Boggs shouted into the phone. The connection was not good.

"Hello. My name is Raj. What appears to be the problem?" The man on the other end of the phone said. Boggs spoke even louder.

"I need. Password reset."

The calm voice, with a thick Indian accent, spoke very calmly.

"This will not be a problem." *It better not be.* Boggs thought.

"For extra verification I will need the last four digits of your social security and your mother's maiden name. After that information has been provided, please tell me your favorite color."

After giving the IT man half of his personal information, Boggs received a newly generated password. One that was so complicated he had to write it down and store the information on to his phone.

Ten minutes later he was dialing Rod.

Brring brring. BRRing BRRing.

The video box opened up.

"Hey, sweetie!" There was Rod, smiling and happy. "How was wine country?"

"Hey, there!", Boggs said, generally happy to see Rod. "It was great!" Holding up his glass of wine to the camera. "What are you up to? Figured I'd call you before you went to bed. Where are you?" Boggs wasn't exactly sure what he was looking at.

"Oh this? This is my home!" *Oh Lord.* "Rustic don't you think!"

God it was awful. That was the truth that Boggs would never admit to. "It's great!"

Behind Rod was a picture of a donkey, obviously drawn by a child. Other than the picture taped to the plaster wall, Boggs saw a decrepit wall of peeling plaster, some cobwebs, and in the corner an old broom.

"Work will be crazy. Can't believe I go back tomorrow."

"So, nothing has changed." Rod had heard this one before.

"Hey, it's not funny. This is for real. The store might close if we don't think of some ingenious way to stay relevant." Boggs was frustrated with Rod's lack of concern. "Let's change the subject. What else are you up to down there?"

"It's awesome. My day starts at 6 a.m. I wake up and this real cute maid fixes me breakfast."

51

"Maid? I thought you were on a mission helping poor people and you have a freakin' maid?!" Boggs couldn't believe what he was hearing.

"Naw, it isn't like that. We're helping her. "

We…Who is WE? Thought Boggs. A pang of jealousy hit him hard.

"Then it's off on the two hour drive to school, dirt roads and wild animals, driving on a tiny bus through the dusty streets of Peru, way up into the mountains."

"That sounds…terrible." Boggs needed to find out who the '*we*' was that Rod was referring to. "So, who is this 'we' you mentioned?"

"Oh, there's just a guy who works here too." Rod said casually, like it was nothing.

Inside, Boggs was burning up. "Tell me more…"

"Just a guy." He changed the subject quickly enough. "So, then I'm at the school and I teach 5 through 9 years old's English. I finish the day at around 5 p.m. and make my way back. Hopefully, I make a difference. So far, I've only been able to teach the kids the words 'beer' and 'retail'. Hey, at least it's something, right?"

"Glad you're making a difference, honey. So, who are you living with?" He'll catch him out perhaps. "What's your place like?"

Rod took his phone and panned the room so Boggs could see his vast living quarters. Rod was hardly slumming it.

"Follow me. This is obviously my room. Then we step out and walk down this corridor and here is the living room." The house where Rod was living was much nicer than Boggs had anticipated. He spotted a Persian rug and some South American antiques.

Outside the two large glass doors at the end of the living room, Boggs spotted a young man pulling weeds in what appeared to be a large leafy garden. The man was young, maybe mid-twenties, and had dark, sexy features. Boggs had to take a closer look.

"Who is that in the garden?", asked Boggs, trying not to sound upset.

"Hey, Jorge. Say hello to Boggs." Rod zoomed in on the shirtless, tanned man, weeds in hand and giant sun hat on his head. Jorge simply nodded obediently.

"What, he doesn't speak? He's mute? Or have you been teaching him other things instead of English?" Failing to hide his distain, Boggs took a drink of wine to calm him down.

"He doesn't speak English. You're so silly sometimes, Boggs. You know I love you."

"He seems nice." Boggs hated to be passive aggressive, but he didn't know to handle his emotions. He was either going to drink more wine or workout at the gym. He decided on the latter and pushed his wine glass to the side.

"He's awesome. Look, here is the garden." It was huge. It was filled with exotic plants and large bougainvillea trees. It looked like heaven.

But Boggs was tormented as hell.

As soon as the call ended, Boggs sat there on his couch and gave himself an inner emotional pep talk.

I will not be down. I am better than this. I got this. I have nothing to worry about.

Then he changed into his workout gear, grabbed the keys, and headed to his car ready for the gym.

TEVI'S COMMITMENTS

Finally, Tevi had been able to leave the department store and was in a limo on route to the airport. It was a fifteen-minute ride that felt like an hour. She couldn't board that plane fast enough. She thought the day would never come. Vacation time was so needed. The HeidtMoore had really taken its toll on her mental health. She had done nothing but work for the past six months and now it was time for some much-needed rest. Her plan was to not think about work, not contact anyone at work and certainly not worry about making sales goals. No way. She deserved this break, and she was going to turn all of her gadgets off so that no one would be able to contact her. Bliss.

Tevi boarded a plane en route to Arizona. She had saved up all her vacation days earned at the HeidtMoore in preparation for two glorious months off work at the famous Commitments Surgery & Day Spa. Commitments was where all the celebrities and anyone with large amounts of money went for nip tucks, drug and alcohol rehab, medi-spa services, and wellness retreats.

Tevi went to Commitments about every three years for wellness and medi-spa services. This year more invasive work was planned as she was scheduled for a complete facelift. Even though she was only in her forties and didn't have any wrinkles, she wasn't taking any chances. It was important to look good at the HeidtMoore.

The resort was just far enough from Dallas for Tevi to relax. Sitting back in her first-class seat waiting for her glass of champagne, she began to wonder who she would run in to this year. During her last visit she saw Mrs. Gottrocks. She never failed to see at least one of her clients there. But it didn't bother her. In fact, she like having something in common with the elite HeidtMoore clientele. It set her apart from the other managers, which she to pride in.

Champagne in hand, reclining in her first-class seat, Tevi opened the personalized Commitments pamphlet and began to review her itinerary for the next two months. The first week she would have the face lift and then spend the rest of her stay recuperating. Maybe she would get a few other things done too? Like bottom enhancement? It was all the rage and if Kylie Jenner could have it done, why shouldn't she?

The flight was smooth and arrived on time. Tevi was pleased as she hated to be late for anything, even if it was completely out of her control. She was not known for her patience. After picking up her luggage at the baggage claim she headed for the curbside car service. The black town car provided by Commitments was waiting. The drive to the resort was just short of an hour from the airport.

Picking up her work phone, Tevi opened the Outlook email app and began to browse through the messages in her inbox. *Ugh, her promise not to open any work-related stuff was already broken!* But she couldn't resist. Just one last look at work stuff before she put it away. It wouldn't hurt. Debating whether to open any more emails and check Spark for sales numbers, she glanced out of the window. The scenery in Arizona was completely different from Dallas. Tevi was already feeling less stressed being away from the store. She decided against opening any of the emails and Spark and switched to Instagram instead. She took a picture of the view outside her window and posted it. #desertlandscape.

Within a few hours, Tevi had settled into her room, which was designed in muted tones, sort of Goop meets monastery. A little too bare for Tevi's tastes. But the finishes and the attention to detail were impeccable. On the nightstand was a note that read:

"Welcome to Commitments, Tevi. May your heart receive anything your soul desires."

After unpacking her suitcase, it wasn't long before she was sitting poolside, ordering her second daiquiri. Prada sunglasses perched on top her head, her fabulous thick jet-black hair piled high into a bun, she reclined on a sunbed with her favorite magazines: Vogue, People and US.

"Can I offer you another drink? Another daiquiri or would you like to try our homemade mango margarita? We grow the mangos onsite." Asked a waitress wearing a bikini.

Oh, what the hell?

"Sure. Why not. I'll try the mango marg."

Scanning the pool area, she was pleased to see there were a few familiar faces. While discretion was paramount, Tevi couldn't resist getting out her phone.

OMG. She texted Mary. *You'll never believe it. Brad Pitt is here. #hot.*

That was just enough information. Pulling her glasses down on her nose, she put her Apple X back in her Valentino straw pool bag and resumed reading US magazine.

Moments later, she looked up again to see a gorgeous hunk wearing a tight Speedo entering the pool area.

He must have been about twenty-three. Much too young for Tevi, but what was the harm in looking? She pulled her glasses to the tip of her nose and peered over the rim. *Wait a moment. Who is that behind the hunk?*

There was someone, another man, behind the young hunk. Someone Tevi thought looked remarkably familiar. But who was he? She looked closer as the two men got settled near the bar area.

"Here is your mango margarita. Enjoy," said the waitress, interrupting Tevi's thoughts.

"Thank you." Tevi took out her Valentino wallet and tipped the waitress ten dollars. Feeling a little lightheaded from the sun, the alcohol and seeing Brad Pitt, it was time to take a dip in the pool.

The pool was a decent size with a giant waterfall at one end and a swim up bar on one side. Tevi almost had the pool to herself as it was nearly empty. The saltwater felt so good. After swimming a couple of laps, Tevi got out of the pool and dried herself off.

Sitting back down on the sunbed, her attention went back to the handsome men who were now near the bar. They were in view and Tevi couldn't believe what she was seeing.

It took a few more moments. Then Tevi sat there…in shock. It couldn't be…it *was*.

It was Mr. Heidt, and he was looking very much alive and well!

Tevi watched closely as the young man in the Speedo and Mr. Heidt ordered a drink. Tevi couldn't move. It was like she was frozen. Should she go over there and talk to him? Was this real? *But he's dead!* That couldn't be him. Or was she just drunk? Tevi took out a bottle of Evian and chugged it down. She didn't know what to do. This was unbelievable. A mixture of emotions swept over her; excitement, joy, anger…how could he make us believe he was dead when in actuality he was at a rehab with some young guy?

She finally took out her phone.

Mary. You will never believe who I've just seen!!!!

SALTY NACHO

Mary was getting ready for her date with Nacho. Nothing special, just heading to Flirty Birds for dinner. This is what she told herself every time she went out with him, *nothing special, just play it cool.* But in reality, her expectations got the better of her.

Looking in the mirror one last time, checking her teeth for lipstick, Mary adjusted her brand-new Veronica Beard dress. Had she made this impulsive purchase in anticipation of tonight's dinner with Nacho? Maybe. Could she afford the dress? Probably not. Thankfully, she just put the dress on her HeidtMoore charge card where she wouldn't have to worry about the charge until the following month. The problem was she always wanted to look good and working in retail made it easy to spend money that she didn't have on clothes she couldn't afford. It didn't matter. She wanted to look good for Nacho.

Another big change was Mary's online status. She had recently changed her Facebook profile to "in a relationship", which meant she had to post proof that she was, in fact, in a serious relationship. There was a push at work to become more "social." Mary found this funny because she was never the social type. But her good friend T was abundantly social. T was always going to events and parties. She was a regular at many restaurants and bars throughout Dallas and she posted every picture online for all the world to see. With her new bestie and a boyfriend, Mary was bound to become "social." She downloaded Instagram, Twitter, Facebook, and YouTube all at once to her phone.

Arriving at the restaurant, Mary was excited to see Nacho. They met at the bar and then proceeded to a table. Nacho, always the gentleman, pulled Mary's chair out before taking his own seat. She loved that about him.

"Can't believe Heidt is back, can you? Crazy." Nacho didn't like to talk about work outside of the store, but this news was so shocking that he couldn't resist.

"I've never even met the man!" The boss Mary was meant to report to, was actually alive and, possibly, coming back to the store. Mary didn't know what to expect. "Tevi hasn't talked to him yet. She was debating whether or not to. My guess is she will have to run into him at some point. Commitments can't be that big."

"Well I'm sure as soon as Heidt sees her, he will contact me. He will want to make sure his privacy is maintained."

"Do you think he will come back to the store?

"We'll see if he even makes an appearance for the big Holiday Hot Chocolate event this season. That's the word on the street. He comes back, the store will be saved, and we won't have to worry about our jobs."

"Worry about our jobs?" This was the first time Mary had heard about this.

"Oh, you haven't heard. There are possible layoffs coming. Don't worry, we're probably not effected. But still…worrying."

"I can't afford to be let go!" She was thinking of all of the new HeidtMoore purchases she had recently made. Mary started to panic and could feel lockjaw coming on. She'd only had a couple sips of her margarita.

"Don't worry. Like I said, we're probably going to be fine since we are managers. They will probably let go of corporate staff in the buying office. You have nothing to worry about." Nacho took Mary's hand to calm her down. She instantly felt better. Maybe now was the right time to tell him about her social "status". She was thankful to have Nacho in her life.

"Guess what? We're official." She said batting her eyelashes, semi seductively.

"Official for what?" He removed his hand from hers.

"Online silly. I updated my profile. We're officially "official"."

"Why would you do that? We don't need to be announcing to the world. What platform did you do that on? Jesus!" Nacho said with disgust in his voice, pushing himself away from the bar table.

"Facebook. Why is it such a big deal to you? Why wouldn't I? I thought that's what we were. So, I changed my status."

"That is the dumbest thing ever." Nacho was mad.

Mary sat there trying to keep her tears from rolling down her cheeks. She couldn't understand why he would behave like this. Was it his macho temperament? Or was he concealing something?

Mary knew an associate whose boyfriend had two, maybe three girlfriends on the side. The associate confided in Mary all her troubles and how she could never post anything about her boyfriend because of his other girlfriends. Mary couldn't understand her colleague would still want to even see this man. But it wasn't her place to judge.

But now she wondered if Nacho had some girls on the side of whom Mary was unaware?

Nacho calmed down a little, enough to explain to Mary that he didn't like his personal business out there on the internet for the world to see. He explained that he liked to keep work life and personal life separate. Mary didn't believe him.

"You keep work separate from your personal life? Then why are you even dating me in the first place? I don't understand why you are getting so mad." Mary said, slightly raising her voice. "Is that why I can't find you online? You have a secret profile or something?"

"No of course I don't! I just don't use Facebook."

That was a lie. Everyone used Facebook. I mean, she was brand new to it, but her peers had told her everyone did it and so should she. It was typical peer pressure and Mary succumbed to it.

"Everyone uses Facebook. What's your name?"

"Er…Nacho."

"Just Nacho?"

"I'm not on it. I'm on Snapchat."

"What's Snapchat?

"You don't know what Snapchat is? Snapchat is where you send messages and then they disappear." Nacho being very private, thought this was ideal. Mary, on the other hand, grew increasingly more suspicious.

"Oh, you like your messages to disappear, do you? How convenient. And who are you writing messages to?"

"Don't do this."

"Do what?" Mary asked innocently.

"Act jealous." Nacho got straight to the point.

"I'm not jealous."

"You are."

"I'm not."

"You are. That was jealousy."

"Why do you say that? I am not jealous! I just don't know why everything has to be such a giant secret!"

By this time, Nacho had paid the bill for their two drinks which had sat there barely touched. It was no good. Mary and Nacho were two people who could not be reasoned with.

NEW NUTTY CUSTOMER

In Boggs' mind, his first week back at work had been progressing smoothly. He was still getting caught up on reports, but he enjoyed being back at the store. It gave him a sense of control. He was surprised how much he was enjoying his alone time at home without Rod. The one thing that he couldn't stop wrestling with were the thoughts of the store's closure. If something at the HeidtMoore didn't change soon, it would be curtains for all.

Boggs needed an amazing idea for the upcoming holiday season. Still wanting to be the next General Manager, he knew if he came up with a plan to take the store out of its seemingly endless troubles, the job would be his!

Looking across his desk, he noticed the store monkey.

"What is it, Curious?" Curious was the store's mascot of sorts, a monkey Mr. Heidt adopted several years ago during a fundraiser. Curious was a smart monkey and often posed in the window displays throughout the store. Boggs continued his one-way conversation with Curious while the monkey munched on a peanut.

"I need something spectacular this season."

Curious paused, looked at Boggs, and tilted his head, then pointed to the bright green trophy on the shelf behind the desk.

"Yes, Curious. It's green." Realizing the time, Boggs got up from his chair and motioned Curious out the door. "Come on friend, let's get this afternoon going."

As Boggs was making his daily rounds throughout the store, he noticed a peculiar client in the men's department. The man had a long grey goatee, twisted at the bottom, and tied with a bow. He also wore a top hat and noticed that behind a pair of round turquoise spectators the man had the most piercing blue eyes Boggs had ever seen. Watching from afar, it appeared this customer was looking for something specific in the necktie department.

"Good afternoon sir, how may I help? You seem to know what you want. I'd be happy to help you. I'm the Assistant General Manager of the HeidtMoore."

"Hi, thank you. Yes, I'm in need of a tie."

"Happy to find one for you. Did you have any in mind? A particular designer perhaps? Maybe a Ferragamo? Hermès?"

"Have any with nuts?"

Boggs wasn't sure he heard correctly. Did this man just say *nuts?*

"Excuse me?" *Was this a joke customer?* Boggs couldn't tell. Luckily, before he had a chance to find out the answer to his question, a sales associate walked up. Boggs quickly passed him on to someone else so he could get back to serious business, like making sure the store was running properly and associates were making sales.

"Ah, yes. Saul, this gentleman here needs a tie."

Saul, another Lifer, well versed in all areas pertaining to suits, was happy to oblige. "Why of course, follow me sir."

Boggs continued his rounds throughout the store. Reflecting back on the customer, he wondered why he would want nuts on a necktie. *That is nuts!* Laughing out loud at his own joke, he regained his composure as soon as he spotted Sloan.

Sloan appeared to also be making the daily rounds. This was a practice put into place by Mr. Heidt Sr. when the store first opened. But when

Heidt Jr. took the reins, the daily check of all things fell to the Assistant General Managers.

Both Boggs and Sloan took their jobs very seriously and each morning they made sure that everything was in check. Though Mr. Heidt had been found alive, it didn't mean he was coming back to the store. As questionable as that was, the battle was still on to be number one and take his spot. They tried to outdo one another on just about everything; on how friendly they could be with the associates and yet maintain seriousness, keeping the store looking great and feeling great, and on sales, and who could get their team to sell the most. Managers could see their competition and most felt that it was exhausting.

Sloan spotted Boggs heading down the escalator, but he was out of sight before he could catch up to him. *What a shame!* Thought Sloan, as he walked over to the Mens area to see what was going on.

As he walked towards ties, Sloan noticed a customer he hadn't seen before, talking to Saul. Since Saul was very select about his customers and only tended to clients with a net worth of one million dollars or more, this was probably one customer Sloan wanted to impress. He would take this opportunity to introduce himself as the acting store manager and tour him around the store.

"Hello. I am the acting store manager, Sloan Garrett. Are you finding everything you need?"

"Oh, I thought I just met you. Yes, thank you. I have what I need. This nice sales associate is helping me. Need me some nuts."

"Some, what? Sorry, you need, what?" Sloan was a bit bewildered.

"Nuts!" Repeated the customer.

"Yes, well, now that you are done here, let me take you to our epicure department on the first floor. You won't be disappointed. Follow me. Thank you, Saul, that's all for now." Sloan handed the customer his business card. Before the customer could explain why he wanted nuts, Sloan was giving him a tour of the store.

"Here is the finest collection of nuts you will find in the world." Sloan said, taking the customer into the world of epicure. He was proud of his store and the merchandise it carried. Every luxurious item was displayed elegantly on glass tables or shelving units made out of marble.

"But are my nuts here?"

"Mr...sorry, I don't know your name." Sloan was somewhat bemused by this man.

"Penkins. Mr. Pandy Penkins. But you can call me Pandy."

"Well, Pandy, I don't know what you are referring to. Your nuts?" Sloan turned a light shade of pink.

"You ain't never heard of 'Pandy's Nuts from Lubbock'? I own the whole darn distribution; national and international." Pandy walked over to a tin of macadamia nuts. He turned the tin around on its side to show Sloan its distinctive PNL logo, small block lettering inside a small outline drawing of a man with a top hat.

Good heavens, this was the nut man himself. Sloan couldn't believe his luck. Of course, he knew about Pandy. Maybe not specifically about Pandy, but he certainly knew about the nuts. They were a top seller for the store.

"You own 'Pandy's Nuts from Lubbock'? What a pleasure to meet you! Anything you need, you have my card." *Cha Ching Cha Ching* 💵 Sloan had hit the jackpot. This was going to be a very lucrative season.

ANSWERED PRAYERS

Mary had not been to mass in weeks due to numerous reasons, all of which Mary's mom found ridiculous. It frustrated her mother to no end that her only daughter, her precious Mary, would drop out of going to church. It broke her heart, and every night before she went to bed, Deloris prayed that Mary would come with her to church every Sunday like she used to.

"Please, mi amor. Come with me."

"Mama, I can't. I told you. I have so much going on. Work is so intense. I'll go with you next week. I promise..." Mary would say, but never followed up on her promise.

It came as a big surprise to both Mary and her mother when, a few weeks later, Mary *did* go to church. This particular Sunday was different. Mary was wracked with confusion about the recent Heidt news. Mr. Heidt was alive. It didn't make sense. The General Manager of the most important department store in the country, if not the world, had faked death and left his empire to crumble. At least that's what it seemed like.

Mary also felt guilty about her fight with Nacho. Maybe she had overreacted and maybe it was wrong of her to have assumed they were committed to one another.

Nacho wasn't the only reason Mary was feeling exceedingly guilty. Deep down, there was another reason that Mary was feeling this way. It was her faith, or lack of it. Her faith had always been such a big part of her life and now she felt that her life was all about material things. She was letting the department store rule her life. How had it come to this? The HeidtMoore was a force that controlled every aspect; the way Mary dressed, her interactions with people, her work ethic – she never stopped working, and was always busy on the hamster wheel of producing sales volumes that were so unrealistic. It was like this monster was controlling her. She wasn't the only one. She had seen her HR manager, Brandi, crumble under the stress of the workload, and Tevi, who had to get away each year to maintain her sanity. The store was a beast. Was this the price to pay for retail?

Walking into her mother's house, Mary passed Samson, her younger brother, on the couch playing a video game.

"Are you ready to go?" she asked him, tousling his hair as she passed. Immersed in the game, he just nodded his head without turning to acknowledge his sister.

"Mama, I'm here. Are you ready?" Mary yelled upstairs.

She wandered into the kitchen, noticing the left-over breakfast on the table. Glancing over at the table she noticed the Juliska plates she had given her mom for Mother's Day. It made Mary smile. She then proceeded to eat what was left of the breakfast burritos. Her mother made the best breakfast burritos on the planet. Unfortunately, Mary did not inherit her mother's knack for cooking. Nor did she have much interest or desire in learning to cook.

"Mi amor, I am so pleased you are joining us today. We have a lot to be thankful for," her mother said as she headed towards the door. Mary felt a pang of guilt arise.

"You look nice mama." Mary said admiring her mother's long floral, slightly faded dress, and matching hat. She always dressed up for church.

"This old thing?" They both laughed.

"Come on Samson, let's go." Mary urged as she followed her mom outside to her mom's car, an old beat up Toyota Camry.

It was a ten minute ride to the church. A Catholic church, just on the other side of town. Mary had been confirmed in this church and it always brought back good memories to her time in instruction, to the funny priest, and to getting to know some of the other confirmands.

Once inside the church, Mary knelt down at the kneeler. *Dear God, please make me a better daughter, and let these issues with Nacho resolve themselves.* Her prayers continued. *Let me be honest, let me know your presence…*

Her prayers were interrupted by the ringing of the church bell indicating the beginning of mass. She rose from her kneeler and looked around to see the congregation scattered throughout the large church. The service was very well attended with at least a hundred people or so.

Then Mary noticed Nacho, sitting a few rows ahead of her pew. She couldn't believe it.

A blessing indeed! Mary thought. *It was a sign!* She had no idea Nacho attended mass. Although he was a distraction, Mary was able to set her thoughts about him aside and focus on the service. When the priest started his sermon, it was like he was speaking directly to her. He talked about divine love and forgiveness. Exactly what she needed to hear!

It was time to take communion. Mary, Samson, and Deloris all lined up at the rail accordingly. Passing Nacho on the way back to their pew, their eyes met. Mary felt her heart flutter. She went bright red and almost tripped getting into her pew, much to the annoyance of Samson, who nearly fell over her.

"Watch what you're doing!" He said. Mary immediately turned to him to make him stop whining.

"Ssh!" She said sharply.

After the service Mary waited in the courtyard with Samson, while her mother visited with the priest.

"First time?" Startled, Mary turned around and saw Nacho.

"Um, no. Well it has been a while." Why was she nervous? Probably due to the perfectly fitted black suit he was wearing. Straight off a GQ ad. *He is so hot.* Mary's mind was racing. She reminded herself that he needed to apologize. "I haven't seen you here before, is it your first time?" Mary asked him.

"No, I've been coming for a few months. I used to go to St. Monica's, but this one is closer, and the times are better with work."

Damn it, if he can make it work, I should to. Mary thought to herself.

Nacho continued, "Hey, listen, about the other day, I'm sorry. I overreacted."

Mary blushed, "It's okay, I'm sorry too." The two of them stood there awkwardly. Then Nacho broke the silence.

"Maybe next week we can go together?"

Mary tried to act cool. "Thank you. I would love that." Thinking to herself, so *would my mom.*

HE'S ALIVE

It wasn't long before the word got out.

To everyone's surprise, Linda Langley, a journalist, put the news on the front page of the newspaper.

MR. HEIDT FOUND. ALIVE.

The store's General Manager had been missing for nearly a year and half and there were many theories as to his whereabouts. Some people said he suffered from a serious illness and could no longer function. Others, who weren't so kind, said he was involved in a Columbian drug cartel. There was also rumor he was transitioning.

"When you say transitioning? What do you mean?" Mary asked Brandi one day as they were walking the store. Mary had hoped that the more she got to know Brandi, the more insight she might gain on how the store operates and what it would take to further her career.

"Like, from a man to a woman. It's like, normal now."

"Nooo!" Mary was shocked. She had never heard about this before.

"You really need to like, get with the program. Mary, I can't believe how naïve you are sometimes. Let's go look at dresses. A new shipment arrived yesterday." Brandi was more interested in shopping and gossip than she was providing Mary with wisdom.

Then there was another rumor circulating that Mr. Heidt had given up all of his belongings and joined a religious sect in Israel. That rumor was somehow less plausible than the others.

The whole case of the missing General Manager had been something of a mystery. What was an even bigger mystery was how the store was managing to keep its doors open to the public!

The article stated he was suddenly found! Alive! In a rehab facility in Arizona!

A couple of paragraphs underneath this astonishing news was an announcement about a potential HeidtMoore collaboration.

WILL A COLLABORATION WITH ANOTHER RETAILER SAVE THE HEIDTMOORE?

"I mean…duh! I knew all along that he wasn't dead," said Brandi, on another occasion during one of her monthly touch-bases with Mary, the smell of alcohol lingering in the air. It was custom for human resources to have these touch base meetings with top performers, managers, and associates. Mary found them to be a waste of time as they typically turned into gossip sessions. But this meeting would be different. Or so Mary hoped!

"I had to tell you. It was weighing on my conscience. I'm glad he's getting help." On the advice of Nacho, Mary let Human Resources know that there had been a sighting. Unfortunately, it was already too late, the press knew already.

It was funny because the whole time that Mary had worked in the store, she hadn't even once seen the elusive General Manager. She was thankful he was alive, but she made it a habit not to get involved in store gossip, of which there was plenty. It was the best decision to come clean about the text from Tevi, although she hadn't counted on the blazing headlines.

"It's a good thing he's alive. Such a shock." Mary was incredibly good at diplomacy.

"Like, yah! You wanna know what else I know about him?"

"No, I mean, yes. What?!" *I just want to discuss getting a pay raise.* Mary hoped this wouldn't last long, it was a desperately inappropriate HR session.

"Heidt is dating a guy who's eighteen! After every Spring season Tevi goes out to some awesome "retreat" in Arizona. And you know that it's not some spiritual guru spa."

"No?"

"God noooo!" Brandi took a giant swig out of her pink Yeti flask before continuing. "No, no she gets her annual nip tuck, fillers, the works." Brandi said with a very knowing look.

No wonder Tevi seemed to never age. Mary had a lot to learn about the ways of the world. Particularly the retail world.

"So, she gets out, all bandaged up, and she walks towards the pool and there he is! Just getting out of AA. Incredible. In the meantime, here we've been, chugging away" at that moment Brandi took another swig from her drink. Mary found the timing kind of funny. "We're just working hard. Busy, busy bees."

"So, changing the subject, can we discuss my raise? I've been working here now for nearly a year and have taken on three times the responsibility that I planned on. I'm not complaining but..."

Brandi didn't have a chance to respond.

Thud. Thud.

There was someone at the door.

"Babe," said a masculine voice from behind the door.

"Who is that? Come in." Brandi was caught off guard. Mary looked at her quizzically.

"Is that...Chef?"

Brandi's cheeks turned pinker than her Yeti flask.

At that moment Chef barged in carrying a tray of chocolate brownies, not realizing Mary was sitting there.

This is awkward.

"I was just, er, leaving." Mary thought she might be wrong, but she could swear that there was something going on between these two. Brandi looked sheepish and Chef looked like he had been caught with his hand in the cookie jar.

Mary quickly said her goodbyes and left them to it. *Well, that was another useless meeting without any sign of a raise or extra help for the busy, and fast approaching, holiday season.*

Chef set the tray of brownies on Brandi's desk. He swooped her up from her chair and began to kiss her neck.

"Stop it Chef, anyone could walk in. It was bad enough Mary was just in here. Not now." She said trying to push him and away with no success.

"Not now, why not now? No one's coming in."

Giggling, Brandi couldn't help letting him undo the first few buttons on her nylon blouse. In between kisses, Chef mumbled into her ear.

"You've been so cool about the thing with Sparkle. It was a dumb night, you know."

Startled by what she heard, Brandi pushed Chef away and re-buttoned her top.

"Excuse me, what did you just say?"

"Awe Babe, you know she means nothing to me."

"Nothing! How can you say that? No. This can't be real." Having a moment of realization. "You're the one? You got her pregnant?!"

"It was one night." Chef said, pleading with Brandi.

"Get out." Brandi pushed him towards the door. Her head spinning.

"Come on, I will make it up to you. Let's talk after work. Enjoy those bars and I will see you at 6."

"Chef. You got her pregnant. How could you do that? She is having a baby! Your baby!"

"We don't know it's mine. I mean..."

"Even if it wasn't that's not the point. You have been seeing someone else behind my back. How could you?"

"It was a mistake. We were drunk. It really did not mean anything. It didn't. I promise. You believe me, right?" Chef looked at Brandi with puppy dog eyes and started trying to kiss her. As Chef advanced, Brandi held out both arms to block his advance. His eyes closed and his fat lips pursed for a kiss. He looked like a fish.

"Get out."

Chef's eyes opened wide. "Baby!"

"I said GET OUT." Brandi shoved Chef towards the door, his hands touching her body. She wasn't having any of it.

Brandi slammed the door shut. *Fat chance of that. I never want to see him again!*

JINGLE JINGLE

It was early September and for Mary it was just a typical day in the Children's department, taking returns, talking to Hispanic nannies, and cleaning up after screaming toddlers.

However, the matter of the HeidtMoore return policy was really getting out of hand. It felt more like the day after Christmas than it did a regular day in September.

"I am so sorry, but we cannot take this back." Mary said politely refusing to take back a soiled Burberry Children's shirt. "Aside from the fact it isn't in resaleable condition, it's also two years old and we do have a strict 40-day return policy. I'm so sorry."

In response, the customer who had approached her with the return shouted out something about what a great customer she was and how she would never shop at the HeidtMoore again. This was so typical, and Mary was over it.

She knew that line, which usually translated to the fact that she was not a great customer at all. It was a known fact that if a customer followed the first line with "I spend a ton of money here," it actually meant the opposite, and probably meant an exceedingly high return rate.

Mary did not break, and the customer stormed off with the soiled Burberry.

Today was different than other days. For the first time Mary had received an email from Mr. Heidt.

Hello Mary,

I understand you manage the fourth floor. Well done. That is an especially important job. Do you have the product you need? I see the Tech and Athleisure areas have been trending well. How many skus of the Burberry sweaters will you be receiving this Fall season?

It shocked Mary to finally be hearing from him. She felt sorry for him, but this was business and she had to be as professional as possible. Other managers and executives in the store had been receiving texts and emails for a week or so, but this was a first for Mary. So strange! She couldn't figure out why. Maybe it was because he hadn't been in the store for so long, but she just didn't know.

Not quite sure how to respond, she marked the email unread as a reminder to come back to it later after she had reviewed the stock inventories he was questioning.

Pietro, the flamboyant Italian visual manager, and his visual team of eight, were busy in Mary's department measuring fixtures and taping down carpet. They never spent this much time in Mary's section of the store, which was fine with her. She liked to be in control of how her floor looked but when visual arrived it was always something of a shambolic mess by the time they left. What they considered 'artistic' Mary sometimes considered unsellable.

From far off, she saw something very unexpected coming out of the freight elevator. The first of the holiday merchandise was starting to arrive. That meant one thing. The holiday music would be starting any day! This meant months of listening to classics such as 'Last Christmas' and remixes of holiday favorites, such as 'White Christmas' and 'Grandma got Run Over by a Reindeer'. It was a depressing thought, and it was only September.

Mary studied the floor, watching a dozen giant gingerbread men and floor to ceiling candy canes spread throughout the department.

Choosing to ignore the messages coming through from Mr. Heidt on her smart watch, she wondered how much holiday was being placed by the visual team. Each year the holiday season seemed to start earlier and earlier. It wouldn't be long before retailers would be promoting Christmas right after Easter. It was absurd. But such was life.

"We have many more canes coming up. Aren't they beautiful? Imported from Switzerland," said Pietro. "Don't worry, the rest of the store gets covered in reindeers, trees and glitter in a few weeks. Aren't you so lucky to come first?"

"Pietro, they are lovely. Why are we beginning to unpack the holidays now?" Mary had been given a date of October fifteenth. This was way ahead of schedule.

"Darling, you are naïve. Have you not seen? We are in dire straits and losing money. The solution? Start Christmas early. At least that was the memo from Mr. Heidt. Trust me, it was a fucking headache to order fifty-five, eight-foot, candy canes. Not my idea of fun." Pietro scorned the job of getting Christmas ready.

A mechanical voice in a faux British accent sounded from Pietro's phone.

Hello chap. You have incoming mail. Mr. Heidt.

"Oh my gosh! What now? I get thousands of emails from him every single day about the set up and where the talking Santas should go." Pietro immediately opened up his phone to send a reply.

"I've suddenly been getting lots of messages from him too. He must be ready to return to the store soon. Glad I'm not the only one behind on emails." Mary sighed. She was back to assisting customers with their immediate needs, like finding the perfect $500 size 4 t-shirt with the word "Dope," or taking back more returns. She sighed again and wondered if this was the place for her.

EMAILS

The afternoon was moving at a glacial pace. This was completely different from the fast pace of Mary's previous day. The fourth floor was doing well, with decent sales and minimal returns. There was a steady influx of customers who were buying, and the associates seemed to have little, to no, drama going on.

Mary sat in her tiny office and checked email. Email was, of course, the main form of communication at the HeidtMoore. Before the days of computers when the HeidtMoore first opened, personal one-on-one communication was one of the key drivers that made the business the best in the industry. In fact, it was a crucial component of what made this particular retailer so special. Mr. Heidt Sr. and Mr. Moore would visit the designers at their showrooms all around the world. They would also host the buyers and vendors at yearly conferences, wining and dining with the most intriguing conversations. That was then.

Now, it was all email, text messages and video conferencing, via Skype, Zoom and FaceTime. Mary thought it interesting that the store was always hosting meetings; from manager start-ups and weekly progress meetings to associate product knowledge trainings (known as PK's) and all store meetings, in hopes of the best communication. Yet, it was the electronic forms that came before and after these meetings to which the people actually paid attention.

Mary browsed the inbox and came across an electronic form that caught her attention: *Mainframe Remediation. The HeidtMoore is moving to the Cloud.*

Opening the email, Mary continued reading:

Our digital environment is expanding with the latest technology, which is more flexible, maintainable, and efficient. Your area may be drastically impacted. Please be patient as the Spark teams are working hard to keep the systems stable. It's just a migration of applications and we have Super Users from different areas of the HeidtMoore to assist with the platforms...

In her head, Mary heard the teacher from Charlie Brown reading the email, "*muah, muah, muah, blah, blah, blah...*" Would this remediation help or cause more problems? No doubt the latter.

Dragging the mouse to the next message from her inbox: *Manager Meeting tomorrow at 4 p.m. has been rescheduled to 4:15 p.m.* Mary wondered if this meeting was even necessary.

Mary heard a ping from one of her phones. She read the incoming text message. It was from T.

Olga has a great dress; you need to check it out.

She responded with a quick thumbs-up emoji 👍

Curious to know what it was, Mary opened up a new text to Olga.

Hi Olga, T said you have a dress to show me? Should I come up to Fine Five?

Mary waited for Olga to respond and resumed scrolling on the computer desktop, an old PC that ran so slowly that Mary wondered how it would handle any of the new tech initiatives.

Moments later the security code on the chain link office door beeped. Since her office also served as one of the stockrooms for epicure chocolates, there was a constant influx of people.

"Mary, Mary, you working now?", said the thick Russian accent coming from outside the office. It was Olga, trying to get through the rackety door, "I have dress." The beeps continued as she pressed the keypad. "I have no code."

Mary walked over to the door. "Olga it's the same code for all the stockrooms. Come on in." Olga practically fell into the office as Mary opened the door for her.

"Mary, this is the best deal. It's the only one. You like?" Olga said in her broken English, holding up a sky blue fitted cashmere dress.

"Is this the Co. one?"

"Co. Yes. Co. It's perfect for you." Co. was the luxury "it" vendor of the season.

"Well, I do need work clothes. Leave it here and I will try it on today and let you know."

"That's fine. I ring you up now."

"No, no not now. Wait. I have a call with Mr. Heidt in five minutes. I can't get to it now. But I'll text you when I'm ready."

"Mr. Heidt? He's back?" Olga looked nervous.

"No, he's not back. It's a Zoom call. Why are you acting funny?" Mary could see the perspiration drops rolling down Olga's forehead. Why was she acting so strange, like she had something to hide?

"Not nervous. Just fine. Nice man. Okay bye." And with that Olga quickly ran away, leaving the $1500 dress on a grey metal folding chair that served as Mary's office chair.

Slightly dreading this call with Mr. Heidt, Mary took a long swig of water from her Swell water bottle and started to dial in for her call. She had received an email message from Mr. Heidt saying he wanted to touch base to find out how the tech and athleisure departments were doing, and what she would be doing to increase sales over the coming months.

Pressing the Zoom app and hitting "join" for the call, it took a few moments before a fuzzy face appeared on the screen. *Was this Mr. Heidt?* It was so hard to tell because the connection was so bad.

"Mr. Heidt? Hello? Can you hear me ok?" It was impossible to tell what the face on the screen was saying.

Mary spoke louder.

"Sorry! Bad connection! What are you saying?" This was awful and so embarrassing. Of all the times to have a bad connection, it had to be now.

Bloop.

The call ended.

Not knowing what to do, Mary sat there in silence debating whether or not to try back. This was so strange. In part, Mary had been excited to get on the call just to be able to see the mysterious General Manager, who had once been her idol. She couldn't believe the interactions the other people in the store had with him via email or Zoom, or even Snapchat.

He did not call back.

Mary decided to try on the dress. She took it off the hanger, took one look around her office to make sure there weren't any security cameras, and then proceeded to strip. She struggled to fit the dress around her hips. *Damn. There must be an issue with the European sizing.*

The dress didn't fit and Mary regretted eating the box of HeidtMoore chocolate chip cookies that had been on her desk that morning. Annoyed, Mary left her office and headed for the stairs in the back hallway.

She walked downstairs to the basement to see what new animals had arrived in the zoo area. That would be a nice distraction from her recent weight gain.

The basement area was open with large cages along the walls. There was a small center court where animal training occurred. There was also an exit door to a small courtyard outside.

"Hi Antonio, any newbies today?" Mary asked as she headed over to the penguin cage.

"Hi Mary, not today. Antonio said, "but the reindeer should be arriving any day."

"Wow, the reindeer." Mary remembered seeing the deer in the windows years ago when she was a child and walk by the store with her mother. That seemed like a lifetime ago. Picking up some feed, she bent down and let the birds eat from her hand. Realizing quickly she had forgotten to put on gloves, she threw the remaining seeds on the ground and watched the birds eat. Antonio had told Mary when the birds arrived that they were a couple, mated for life. *I wonder if Nacho wants a mate for life?* Watching the penguins took Mary's mind off of things only for a bit.

ZAP! CLANK! BOOM! "Shit!" Antonio yelled.

Mary startled by the loud noise, yelled back, "Are you okay? What the hell was that?"

"Another breaker just broke. You know the entire store's electrical system is down here. One day it's going to explode if they don't update it."

Hearing these words Mary thought of the *remediation email.*

"Antonio, you know everything is going to the cloud anyway." Mary sounded as if she knew what she was talking about.

"Mary, that's all the internet stuff, not the actual electricity to run all those computers, POS stations, and lights for this place."

"Oh. Well," trying to hide her terror, "I'm sure they will update all of that also," pointing to the big gray box on the wall that was smoking. "I better get back upstairs. Hope it's not another blackout," she said half-jokingly.

"Not funny." Antonio replied, but Mary didn't hear as she was already out the door.

DEATH OF A SALESWOMAN

To take her mind off work, the abundance of electronic communications (especially from Mr. Heidt), the holiday setup, and the threat of financial ruin for the HeidtMoore, Mary decided to take herself to see a play. Her client had given her tickets to see "Death of a Salesman" starring Chris Pratt, whom she loved. This would be a wonderful evening, calm and relaxing and quite different from her usual nights spent at home cooking, reading, or watching a sitcom.

As soon as she got home from work, she took a quick shower and walked into her Cloffice to pick out something elegant for the special night at the theatre. *How fun!* She couldn't wait. Deep down she wished Nacho could be with her. She needed to not think about him, or the fact that he hadn't called her. Men were ridiculous. She didn't need him. She was perfectly fine to go out on her own.

She drove downtown and parked her car a few blocks away from the theatre. Walking down the road she noticed several couples taking an evening stroll, laughing, looking so in love. Would she ever be like them? With Nacho? Only time would tell. Getting into the theatre she found the usher who took her to her seat, third row center from the stage. *Wow this was great!*

83

With five minutes before the curtain call, Mary glanced around to see who was in attendance at the theater. Much to her amusement she saw Mrs. Ivory, the HeidtMoore's top client, and wife of the Texas senator. Mary recalled the handbag incident of the previous season. It was a close call that they retrieved her one-of-a-kind handbag. Interestingly she was with a gentleman, slightly younger than her fifty-five years. It wouldn't have mattered who she was with except for the fact that she was certain that she saw Mrs. Ivory holding the gentleman's hand. Now that would be a scandal!

Mary looked the other way in slight embarrassment and almost immediately was distracted by yet another HeidtMoore client. It was Mr. Gottrocks senior. Mary could not imagine, not for one second that Sparkle could be his daughter-in-law. That is, if the rumor were true that Gottrocks Jr. was the father of Sparkle's child. It was too much to fathom.

An announcement was made. *Please turn off all cell phones and pagers.*

Mary felt butterflies in her stomach, so excited to see a live show. Starring her favorite actor! She didn't know anything about the play. She had chosen not to read about it so she would be completely surprised. However, she did know it was highly acclaimed, and written by the man who was married to Marilyn Monroe.

The curtain rose and the actors appeared on the very bare set.

About ten minutes in, Mary wondered if anything would happen. It seemed to be a little slow and she had to fight to keep her eyes open. It really had been such a long day. *Why was the HeidtMoore sucking the life out of her?* Mary keenly observed the set. The design wasn't very inspiring. Lots of grey and brown to express the depressing state in which the "salesman", Willy Loman, found himself. She understood that feeling. His two sons were slobs and Mary couldn't help but think of her own brother. He wasn't really a slob, but a pain in the neck, so she could relate.

As the show progressed, the mood of the play didn't. It was bleak, and Mary's mind kept wondering back to the worries of work. The lack of sales, the troublesome clients – some of whom were in the room that she had to deal with, the giant sales goals and the holiday season. It felt like it was going to be one giant train wreck.

Word of a collaboration was spreading throughout the store, but Mary could not see how this could possibly work. A discount retailer and the HeidtMoore? It didn't make sense. Was the store that desperate to stay afloat they were willing to try anything? Uncertain of her future, she looked at the actors on stage and saw her own sad predicament. There was Willy Loman, the main character, having lost his identity, lost in a maze of failed hopes and dreams. Mary had hopes and dreams. What were they? Was it too late? Fashion editing! A fashion magazine! The maze of the HeidtMoore had sucked her in. There was no escape....

Suddenly Mary woke up to the wild round of applause. She had slept through much of the second act. The play had ended. The curtain was falling. The only person on stage was the lifeless body of Loman. What a downer.

Mary was happy to go home.

Once home, she poured herself a glass of red wine and ran a hot bubble bath. She needed to relax. That had been a remarkably stressful evening of "entertainment." From now on she would stick to watching Netflix.

SPECIAL ORDER HOLIDAY

The following day, Mary arrived promptly at work to see what new chaos the day would bring. Several new fixtures had arrived at the store; a giant talking Santa on the first floor in Cosmetics, two singing reindeer in the Ladies Shoe department and a fake chimney smack in the center of the Gifts & Home floor.

"What on earth…!?" Mary's mouth fell open in disbelief as she finally reached her floor. *Why was there so much holiday coming through the store? It was only September!*

From out of nowhere, Boggs jumped up behind her, startling her.

"You just wait till Santa comes down the chimney. This is going to be a Christmas no one will forget. Mark my words, Mer, we have something else in the works. Something b.i.g." He then gave her a shotgun by clicking his fingers and pointing his forefinger at her.

"But how are we going to sell around the chimney, the giant gingerbread men, the huge Santa, and the candy canes and reindeer? Not to mention, summer isn't even over yet."

"Hey, hey, relax. You got this. Oh, look who it is, isn't she wonderful?" Boggs spotted Mrs. Ivory walking across the Athleisure sales floor. She looked elegant in her cream-colored Chanel suit and double strand of freshwater pearls. Boggs waved at her, then turned to Mary.

"Well, Mer, I gotta go. Helping Visual set up lights and the tinsel for the Christmas trees in Men's. They were delivered today and are the biggest trees we've ever had. Take care of Ivory." Why Boggs had to always remind Mary of things she obviously already knew drove her insane. "Take care of Mrs. Ivory, okay? She's our top client. You got this." He gave her another shotgun click of the fingers and left the selling floor.

Did he forget that the previous season it was Mary who helped make the big sale happen for Mrs Ivory, by retrieving a missing one-of-a-kind Ostrich bag, even though she wasn't even her client?! Boggs drove Mary nuts sometimes. Now she was irritated and wanted very much to go back to her office and do office work instead of being on the floor.

Just when Mary's morning couldn't get any worse, she had to help Mrs. Ivory, which was always an ordeal. It wasn't that she was a terrible person. On the contrary, she was rather nice but there wasn't a single order Mrs. Ivory placed that didn't come with complications. Mary also didn't want to go through a discourse of the play from the previous night.

"Was that you I saw in the audience?" Not leaving Mary any room to reply to her question. "Didn't you just love it? A bit sad, but so profound!"

"It was an enjoyable evening, for sure." Mary had been raised to always be truthful. In this instance, she focused on how enjoyable the evening it was once she returned home. She even had a slight headache from the wine. Trying to change the subject, Mary asked, "Anything I can assist you with today?"

"Yes, I have a list of five hundred and fifty people I need Christmas gifts for. It's for my husband's staff so nothing too expensive. We don't want to set the bar too high if you know what I mean." Mary took the list and glanced over the names. She was impressed that Mrs. Ivory was so organized and getting to her list early, but on the other hand Mary felt it was still a bit soon. Halloween had not even happened yet! It was going to be a long day.

Mary browsed the Gifts & Home floor for inspiration. Once she had a few ideas in mind for the gifts, she went to her office to compose an email to the buying office.

"Hi Hayley, would a special order of the mini Jay Strongwater pieces be ready by mid-November? Quantity 500, all engraved. Please confirm and I will send the order through. Thank you!"

A few hours later a reply, "Hi Mary, yes, of course, I've marked style -JSMini- for your store. Send the order through."

Mary had found gifts for all five hundred and fifty of Mrs. Ivory's husband's staff. Small diamond encrusted picture frames, each one to be individually engraved with the name of the recipient. Mrs. Ivory was thrilled. Mary was thrilled to have the large sale for the day. Now she just prayed the follow through would happen. It wasn't a complete sale in Mary's eyes until the gifts received. They also had to be checked for errors, gift wrapped immaculately, and delivered to the correct addresses. And, of course, paid for in full, and with no returns. At any point in this process things could, and often did, go wrong.

"Oh darling, you are divine. Thank you. Oh, and by the way, I was with my friend in the audience. He's my friend if you know what I mean so discretion is advised. Also, I'd like you to find something I can give him for Christmas. Tootles!" Mrs. Ivory turned and walked away.

Why was the senator's wife confiding in Mary?

BIG COLLAB

The morning meeting took place shortly after the scheduled time of 10:00 a.m. Apparently there had been some hiccup with the surprise guest Boggs planned to introduce and so the time was moved to 10:30 a.m.

Mary was hurriedly running to the escalator, not wanting to be late for the startup meeting when Nacho literally bumped into her.

"What's the rush?"

"I just don't want to be late. You know how Boggs is. One minute late and he makes you recite a whole weeks' worth of sales numbers to the tune of Michael Jackson's *Beat It*. I mean, really? It is terrifying. He thinks it's awesome."

"For sure, ha ha. Don't sweat it though."

"Why do you say that?" Mary asked.

"Just got a text. It's been pushed back thirty minutes."

"What! Why am I always the last to know?" *This was so typical.* Mary thought.

"Nah. No worries. We may as well grab a quick coffee. What do you say?"

"Sure! I'd love to!" said Mary, a little too eager. "I mean, that's fine. Why not?" Mary couldn't believe it. She said trying to brush it off like she was cool.

Over coffee in the Pingüino, Nacho and Mary talked about her desire to move up in the company. Unfortunately, every time Mary went to lift her coffee cup her hands shook so much, she had to hold the cup with both hands.

"Do I make you nervous?" asked Nacho.

"Don't be silly! Of course not." Although Mary actually didn't doubt it. "Low blood sugar that's all."

At 10:30 a.m. that morning, the majority of managers assembled in the executive office for the big announcement. It was true, the notice of a collaboration in the local newspaper had not been mere gossip.

Boggs was so eager to let everyone know he was practically jumping up and down on the spot. Standing beside him was a large man in overalls and a bright pink Hawaiian shirt. His leathery skin showed signs of years spent on a ranch or doing heavy construction work.

"He looks really familiar. Can't quite put my finger on it." Sam whispered to Sarafina.

"Don't look at me. I have no idea."

Once the managers were settled and quiet, Boggs began with his introduction.

"I am so excited to introduce Mr. Nickels of the famous and well respected C.J. Nickels department store!"

A few managers exclaimed *ahhhs* and *oooohs* over their guest, having now put the face to the name.

Sarafina whispered to Mary, "Well respected if you shop at Walmart."

Mary raised her eyebrows in disbelief. Nothing against Walmart or lower priced retailers. She liked them and she had shopped there with her mother for as long as she could remember, but this was the HEIDTMOORE. What was the connection? It was just plain weird. She was also very curious to know why a lower price retailer was being introduced to the team in the HeidtMoore executive office. It made no sense. They had two completely different customer bases.

Then the retailer spoke. His deep southern drawl became very apparent.

"Hey, y'all. We're real happy to be here at this fine establishment. The HickMoore."

"Er, HeidtMoore." Boggs interjected.

"Yeah, it's real nice. Classy. Our customer base is big. Real big. We're gonna provide y'all with a taste of the fast fashion. We currently service thousands of customers a day. Our whole thing is lower price point goods that everyone will want."

"Tevi is not going to like this one bit." Mary whispered to Sarafina.

"I can tell you right now that my team will quit when I tell them who we are going to be doing business with. This is a huge mistake for the company. Huge."

"Oh no, come on. They won't quit.", said Mary reassuringly, to which the PJ manager simply raised an eyebrow.

Mr. Nickels continued, "Who knows our store?" No one raised a hand. "Real good. So, I opened my first store in California when I was twenty, because there wasn't anywhere that sold nice stuff at a low price. I've made a fortune. A nickel here a nickel there," he laughed.

It was time for Boggs to step up and say something.

"Guys. This is going to be huge. This will be our biggest event of the season. Got it? Huge! We are going to attract so many people. We are opening doors with this collab. A whole new clientele for your associates."

"What happens to the current clientele?"

"Nothing. That never will change."

"What will be included in this collaboration?"

"What *won't* be included in this collaboration?! We have a fine assortment of merchandise both from Nickels and HeidtMoore just in time for the holiday season. From tea towels to ball gowns."

"That's right." Mr. Nickels chimed in.

"Every item from Nickels will be paired with an exclusive HeidtMoore item to match. And the best part? Every piece will be under $150."

"That's the best part?" Sarafina asked. This was not going to go well for associates. How would they meet their sales goals when they were used to selling an average price point per item of $2000?

"Actually," Boggs continued, "each item will be recycled, part of our 'Be Clean Go Green' initiative. All of the materials are made using sustainable products."

"Like what?"

"Good question. Sarafina. Well, we have," Boggs wasn't entirely sure, "we are about radical transparency. We use clean silks, our bags will be made from spun yarn, sanitized wool pieces and other neat things."

"Talk about being nickel and dimed." The crowd, except Mr. Nickels and Boggs, snickered.

"Any questions?" Boggs scanned the room. Spotting Mary with her hand half raised. "Yes Mary. Shoot!"

"When will this event take place?"

"We're working out the logistics, but we're looking at the week of Thanksgiving."

Each manager left the room wondering how on earth this collaboration was going to work. Mary texted Tevi about this new initiative as she was walking out. Tevi responded only with a thumbs down emoji. 👎

Two weeks later a few boxes of Nickels/HeidtMoore merchandise began to arrive. They were a couple of days late and the executive team had started to panic.

The shipping team in the basement of the department store started vigorously unpacking and unfolding the items. Unable to decipher exactly what they had received, they found amongst other things fifty hand crafted soap dishes made from lemons. *Soap dishes?* Another box contained two hundred dresses made from black trash liners, tied together with the exclusive label reading '*C.J Nickels loves HeidtMoore*'.

"Who the heck is going to purchase these things?" asked Willy, the shipping and receiving manager, to no one in particular.

"Around here they'll buy anything. You know what our customers are like. Remember last season when we sold out of the Hudson Hawn onesies?" replied Nacho, who was referring to the unique line of onesie garments Goldie Hawn and Kate Hudson were selling.

"How could I forget? I thought if I had to receive on another box of celebrity onesies, I'd jump off a cliff."

The customers of the HeidtMoore, the high net worth customers, were a formidable clientele; senators, movie stars, royalty, rock stars, socialites…and all ridiculously hard to please. They had egos to match their back accounts, which were huge.

The problem was the designated sales associates who waited on these illustrious characters acted more like divas than the customer. It was a real nightmare and often led to a lot of unnecessary drama. Asking them to sell "Be Clean, Go Green" was going way out of their comfort zone.

Nacho and Willy had just unpacked the last box of merchandise. They took a moment to catch their breath.

"Never received so many boxes in one day. Phew. Glad that's over."

"Thanks. Really appreciate. You know, I need to ask you something," Willy said conspiratorially "I heard the news that Chef might have gotten one of our associates pregnant? Heard it from someone in Shoes."

"You know I don't gossip Willy," said Nacho, always the professional.

"Come on man, you know everything." He said, slapping Nacho on the arm. "You gotta know who it is."

Even if Nacho did know, he wouldn't be telling Willy.

BEAUTY BOTS

During Tevi's extended vacation, Sloan hired an assistant for her, in the Cosmetics department.

He still had not found the right person to manage only the Cosmetics area. While Tevi had been doing a good job, he knew he needed a full timer, someone completely dedicated to beauty. He also went ahead and hired a dozen other new associates. Normally, hiring was done through the HR department, but these were not normal associates. They were *BB's*. Beauty Bots. Robots! They were first introduced to Sloan and Boggs during their visit to C.J. Nickels. Surprisingly, Sloan and Boggs both agreed they were amazing. Since the Cosmetics department was under Sloan's realm, he was left in charge of getting those BB's to the HeidtMoore.

There they stood, all in line just in front of the LaMer counter. Twelve white robots with heads that looked human, arms, chest, and torso in shiny white metal. Below the waist a cased-in computer system on wheels. At the head of the line, was the assistant BB. This bot looked the same but was cased in shiny black metal with steel accents. She also hovered a good 6 inches higher than the others.

Unbelievable! Mary thought as she stood in awe with the other managers. They had moved their morning start up to the Cosmetics department for the big debut.

"They are all on time for work and ready to go."

Rumblings from the other managers were difficult to decipher. As Mary was trying to focus, she was startled when the Assistant BB started speaking, literally, like a human. Her voice was clear, loud yet soothing, at the same time.

"Welcome to the HeidtMoore, I'm ABBI." Said the eager beauty bot. ABBI, Mary would later find out stood for Assistant Beauty Bot Intelligence.

As soon as the PK adjourned, several terribly upset cosmetics associates stormed upstairs to Human Resources.

Bang. Bang.

They pounded the door to Brandi's office.

Zane led the pack ahead of the others. He had worked at the HeidtMoore for twenty years and wore lots of bronzer. His jet-black hair slicked into a coiffure. A sort of modern day, gay, Elvis.

"Where are you, Brandi?" The question went unanswered.

"Are we getting fired? How could they do that?" A very worried make-up artist tugged on Zane's jacket.

"Stop! I'm wearing Tom Ford!" Shielding his jacket away from the associate, pushing her off of him and jumping aside, literally, to avoid his colleague's touch. "We are not getting fired damn it. Over my dead body! Brandi, are you in there?"

Brandi was under her desk. Sleeping. Her pink Yeti flask beside her. She stirred ever so slightly. It had been a long morning. She had sent Chef on his way, making sure he would never work at the HeidtMoore ever again. She should never have had an affair with him, but she couldn't resist. He had a raw magnesium with his burly body, hot and sweaty from being in the kitchen. He was like a giant bear and made Brandi feel sexy. But that was in the past. Those days were gone. He had cheated on her and made her feel cheap. Why did he have to go and screw everything up? Why? Now…alone, she felt she had no anchor. Had she really fallen for him? She was a mess. Her makeup smeared across her face, alcohol on her breath, and the constant…banging. *Oh my gosh, make it stop.* Brandi's head was spinning.

Who was banging on her door now?

Brandi slowly got up off the floor, pulled out an Estée Lauder compact and stared blankly into the mirror.

The banging continued. She got out a hairbrush from her oversized pink patent leather Gucci bag and dragged it through her bleach blond shoulder length hair. She popped a breath mint into her mouth and staggered over to the door.

Before she could even open the door, Zane barged in, followed by the others.

"How could you? You have betrayed us!" He was mad and waving his hands about.

"What are you talking about?" She generally had no idea.

"The beauty bots! How could you?" Associates behind Zane started crying. Brandi sobered up pretty quickly and composed herself.

"Let me explain. Yes, we have beauty bots and no, you don't have anything to worry about."

"I thought I would never see the day when we would hire ROBOTS as…as…as makeup artists!"

"White robots too!" said Shirley, a beauty vendor in her seventies.

Another associate chimed in.

"I thought we were an inclusive company."

"You didn't hire black, brown or yellow robots," said another.

"Yeah!" Everyone other than Brandi appeared to agree with this statement.

"We have many different kinds of robots. Not just white, Shirley." *This had better not turn into a race issue,* thought Brandi. It was one thing to discuss the issue of the bots, but to insinuate that the HeidtMoore was somehow racist in its hiring process was too much. Brandi needed another drink.

"Well everyone. Get back to the floor. We've got sales to make, goals to keep." Feeling tired and needing a pick-me-up, Brandi shooed everyone out and with a sigh of relief closed the door behind them. It was time she left the office. It had been quite the morning, between the beauty bots, anxious employees and firing Chef, Brandi was on the verge of a nervous breakdown. She picked up her pink Louis Vuitton wallet and stuffed her empty yeti flask into her Gucci bag and left the office.

She stumbled out through the store and down the employee backstairs. She had spent many an elicit tryst with Chef in the back stairwell. The memories came flooding back and Brandi started to cry.

What she thought was the door to the outside parking lot turned out to be a giant room filled with dozens of rods of couture. Gorgeous gowns and jewelry cases. How had she gotten so lost? Was she so drunk she didn't know where she was? The vast room contained more designer clothing than most stock rooms. What was this? Desperate to get out of the store, Brandi left the room and managed to get to Flirty Birds without any further interruptions.

Meanwhile, the news of the BB's had spread and nearly everyone was in the cosmetics department watching these "new associates" in action.

"Well Heidt Sr. would be rolling in his grave if he saw this," exclaimed Sam to Sarafina as they watch a BB sample some eye cream on a customer.

"I don't know, they are kind of neat. I mean you don't have to make small talk or worry about remembering who you shopped with."

"Exactly, Heidt Sr. built this place on customer service and exciting conversations."

"Sam, not everyone can turn an alteration fitting into an afternoon of shopping where the customer buys an entirely new wardrobe she didn't even know she needed."

"You're right, it is a talent," Sam laughed as they hopped on the escalator.

TECH TRANSFER

The beauty bots weren't the only upsetting new development for associates at the HeidtMoore.

Today was the day when all the one thousand two hundred and ninety-nine computers, registers and iPhones would be upgraded and transferred to a new "advanced" system. The new systems were to be installed to enhance the customer experience and take the HeidtMoore into the new age.

Of all the department stores, Staks, Lacey's, even CJ Nickels, the HeidtMoore was the last one to adapt to new forms of technology and embrace the online competition. It was really a case of *too little too late* and had led to, among other things, the ten billion dollars worth of debt that the store had accumulated.

"Hey there. I'm looking for Mr. Heidt and the training room," said the tall man approaching the reception area of the executive office. T, the executive assistant, had never met this man, and was slightly taken aback that a stranger was entering her space.

"Mr. Heidt is not here but he is available by text. The conference room is at the end of the hall. I'm sorry, who are you?" After the active shooter incident that happened the season prior, T could never be too sure.

"Yeah, I'm the guy, the trainer, teaching y'all the new 2020 platform on Speedthru."

"On what?"

"Speedthru. It's the new operating system that 2020 will be running on."

Great. Just what the HeidtMoore needs. A system no one knows anything about or will ever want to learn. T tried her best to sound excited and then wondered if he was married.

It had been months since T's last relationship, and she didn't want to be alone anymore. After her failed marriages, she still held out hope for the man of her dreams. People always told her he could come into her life at any time, at any moment. Maybe this was such a moment? Her knight in shining armor was disguised as a corporate technology wizard. Not really T's idea of fun, but she had to keep an open mind. She was also dying of boredom in her role as executive babysitter for the store.

"May I show you the way?" she said seductively, crossing her legs, letting her knee length Prada skirt rise up her thigh.

"Sure. I'd like that. Hope you will be participating in the training. There is one at 10:00 a.m. and another one at 3:00 p.m. They last for four hours."

T almost choked. That sounded awful.

"Of course, I'll be there. I want to learn all about this new technology. It sounds so exciting." That was a blatant lie. T had no interest, knowing full well, from one of her friends who worked in corporate, how much money the company had put into this project. If it were like other projects and initiatives, it would be here today and gone tomorrow.

T walked the trainer to the conference room, which was only two rooms down the hall from where T sat. They passed the Keurig machine.

"Mind if I grab an espresso," said the trainer.

"Not at all. Let me make one for you. What's your flavor? We've got toffee spice, dark roast mango, kimchi light tea, and dark roast."

"Think I'll just do the dark roast."

"Good choice."

As the coffee brewed, T glanced at the trainer. He was handsome, tan, tall and smart. Very into his job.

"I take mine dark." T handed him the coffee and watched him head into the conference room to set up his training materials. He pulled out his Apple laptop from his designer briefcase and ten pens of varying sizes and colors.

At ten minutes to ten, managers started trickling into the conference room. The trainer introduced himself.

"Hey y'all. I'm the trainer. Adam. I'll be introducing 2020, Speedthru, getting you installed and up and running with GI Bot Smart. Any questions?"

"G.I. What?"

"Bot smart. So, you have several bots, and you can program them to pixelate, diminish, embellish any blemish."

Mary sat there. Stifling a yawn. She just wanted to sell and manage her departments. Why was the store becoming an Apple/retail tech hub? Retail was completely changing. And not for the better. She wasn't the only one who felt that way. Looking around, she saw several other managers with glazed looks, completely unresponsive to Adam.

"Get out your iPhones." Instructed Adam.

The managers did as they were told, although most were already swiping through their news feeds on Instagram, Facebook, and Twitter.

"Great. You should have already downloaded app 2020. Raise your hands if you have done that already."

Not a single hand raised.

"Alright. So, let's start there. Access your "Moore apps with Heidt", one of the digital resources on hand for the associates, and you will see an icon with '2020' on the widget. Once there download and open 2020. Sign in with your Heidt account and hopefully you remember the password. Has everyone done that?"

No one answered back.

"Now" Adam continued, "you see a small HM icon on the far right? Click on it and it will enter the main page. This is where all your client's information will be stored. Everything from the last item they purchased, to where they ate dinner the night before."

"That sounds creepy," Hilz blurted. She was never one to hold back. "What else does this do?"

"So much more! This is a game changer in an ever-evolving industry. You will have the resources to everything and anything your clients would want or need. Together we are transforming the retail industry." Then he pulled out a handkerchief from his breast pocket and wiped away perspiration from his brow. He reminded T of an evangelical preacher, preaching the prosperity gospel.

When the meeting finally ended it was just T and Adam in the conference room cleaning up.

"It's such a shame Mr. Heidt couldn't join the presentation. I know he's really is into this stuff." T was trying to get a conversation going.

"Well, he will experience it soon enough. That is the great thing about 'Speedthru', you can access it anywhere," Adam replied.

"I am really excited to learn more," T lied and could feel her cheeks getting hot. "Make sure I have your card because I know I will be the one everyone will come to with questions."

"Sure. I have some cards and information in the car. Do you want to walk down with me?"

"I would love to!"

HOLIDAY INSTALLATION

The State Fair in Dallas was just setting up and Halloween and Thanksgiving were right around the corner. But at the HeidtMoore, Christmas decorations were already delivered and being hung throughout the store. This was retail and the regular rules didn't apply, especially at the department store level.

The HeidtMoore, along with all the other large department stores set up holiday months before the actual day of celebration. This was one of the many things Mary felt was not planned well. For a store of this caliber Mary was shocked when it was announced at the manager meeting that this was the week for the trees to go up. She had just gotten used to the winter wonderland in her Children's department and could not imagine the entire store decked out in garland and lights.

The newest managers to the HeidtMoore were selected as 'elves' for the installation event. This really meant they were the ones who had to come in extra early to help with the setup. The 'Lifers' were excused as they had done their fair share of Christmas decorating over the years and most of them would probably break a bone if they were asked to climb a ladder.

Hilz managed to squeeze herself into the *Lifer* category claiming the years spent in the buying office counted. Mary was not sure she felt that was fair, but what was she to do? She was definitely an elf this year.

Arrival time was set for 5 a.m. T had emailed all the managers the previous day that they could come in athleisure wear and they had to make sure it wasn't an outfit the employees would mind getting sprayed with glitter. Mary arrived on time, latte in hand, not knowing quite what to expect.

"Hey, Mary. Boggs left this box for you," said Brad, assistant loss prevention manager, showing her a medium size box behind the glass partition.

There was a note on top of the box.

Mer, check out these awesome outfits I got for you. Shoot you an email later with explanation.

This did not bode well for the day.

Mary checked her email and sure enough, there was Boggs's email, explaining that he had ordered elf outfits for the managers to wear for the holiday setup. There were sizes small, medium, and large, so there wouldn't be a problem with any of the managers finding the right size.

This was mortifying. Mary did not want to spend the day dressed as an elf!

Opening the box, she took out a red and green elf outfit with sewn in red socks to match. *Why?* Boggs did not need to turn a bad situation into a dramatic event. Mary wondered how she would explain this to the other managers.

As soon as she entered the store through the employee entrance, Mary felt she had entered a different planet. It was a veritable forest of Douglas Firs and Norway Spruce trees. Around the corner, by the freight elevator, were floor to ceiling ornament balls in various sizes from basketball size to giant ones even taller than Mary herself. Just past the doors to the cosmetic floor there were a zillion boxes labeled "Lights." Mary could not believe what she was seeing. She headed toward the winding escalators.

"Pietro, what the hell? Be careful!" Mary yelled as she witnessed Pietro dangling from scaffolding surrounding the giant aquarium.

"Don't worry, I am the lucky one who gets to hang the lights around this atrocity," he replied. "And just wait until you see the epicure department!" Noticing Mary juggling her latte and a massive box, "Need a hand carrying that box?"

"Nope. I'm good. Just carrying a bunch of elf outfits. Nothing to see here," said Mary rolling her eyes.

As Mary carried her box onto the escalator to the 4th floor, she was in awe of the scenes on each floor she passed. Every member of the shipping department and restaurant staff was on hand and each person was either decorating a tree or unloading large cannisters of popcorn and other holiday treats all with the exclusive gold *HeidtMoore for the Holidays* packaging. Exiting the escalator, Mary bumped into Sloan.

"Good morning Sloan, where shall I start?"

"Hey Mary, why don't you start with the trees in the tech area. The ornaments all have batteries, so good luck with that," he replied. Mary's smile instantly became a frown. "But first, you had better distribute those holiday outfits. And don't forget to wear yours!" Giving Mary a wink.

"I've never seen anything like this!" Mary stated.

"You'll enjoy it. They'll look great!"

"Are you kidding? So, you'll be wearing one, right? Mary said knowing full well he wouldn't be caught dead being dressed as an elf.

"Too bad, actually I won't be. Sad but they didn't have one that fit." He held out his belly for extra emphasis. "This is a first this year with the real trees, you know."

"Really?" Mary was surprised.

"Yeah, part of Boggs' 'Be Clean Go Green' initiative," he said, narrowing his eyes and pursing his lips. "I guess we are taking them all to the zoo in the new year. If they last that long,"

Mary distributed the elf outfits to the managers and squeezed into hers. There was only a small left and despite all attempts to get out of wearing one, she walked out onto the floor to start her work inserting batteries into the ornaments.

Brad was walking the floors, doing his usual security checks. He spotted Mary and grinned.

"Nice outfit!"

"Fuck off Brad" Mary wasn't having any of it. She sat down, surrounded by hundreds of ornaments, in the Tech section and went to work installing the batteries.

Five hours later, twenty managers were dressed as elves, and nearly 700 trees had been lit and decorated all over the store. Mary was absolutely exhausted and dying to get out of her sweaty, red and green, synthetic elf costume, that she accidently ripped while getting up from the floor.

The trees accurately represented each area: Heaven or Hell in Intimate Apparel had angels and latex ornaments. The trees in handbags, ladies' shoes and jewelry areas were Mary's favorite: mini Louboutin's, YSL handbags, and tourmaline gemstones adored every tree. Anyone who loved fashion would simply have to purchase something. It was impossible not to as everything looked absolutely magnificent.

Having changed into regular clothes, meaning a simple Valentino sheath dress, Mary sat in her office away from the hustle and bustle of the store. She was exhausted. Sipping the last drops of her now cold latte, she picked out some glitter from her hair. The sad part was that the day hadn't really even started. She still had a few minutes until the store opened and the startup meeting began.

Later that afternoon, T was swiftly darting through the store with her latest tech gadget. She had nearly mastered making promotional movies and was gathering footage of the final holiday set up. She knew either Boggs or Sloan would want a video for the back-hallway TVs and for the morning meetings. It seemed everything they did lately revolved around digital communication. T was not sure it was actually effective but went along with it anyway. *Hopefully, it will lead to a promotion!*

"Mary, is Lulu here today? I need some video footage."

"You think Lulu is the best person for that?"

"Customers adore her! And her co-workers know she is a permanent fixture here and has great stories about Heidt Sr. I am doing a piece that reflects how Heidt Sr. started the HeidtMoore and the first Christmas angle."

"Oh, that is a great idea. You should interview my mom. You know Deloris reminds me all the time how she brought me to see the windows when I was a child."

"That's right! Didn't she and Heidt have a thing way back then?"

"I think they went on one date. You know, before *On the Rocks* was invented," Mary replied laughing at her dating app joke. T rolled her eyes and continued on through the store with her camera.

GROUPIES

Mary was now accustomed to the retail work week. Tuesdays and Wednesdays were normally the slowest days of the week. Fridays and Saturdays were the busiest. However, this Friday afternoon the store was particularly quiet. This was becoming more and more a regular occurrence. Traffic still had not picked up to where it was in previous years. *A sign of the times,* Mary guessed.

Associates stood idly by one of the POS stations in Mary's department. Since there were no customers, Mary decided to go back to her office and check email.

The first email she opened had a message in the subject line that read: WELCOME TO GROUPIES.

WTF is the email about groupies? She texted T.

Immediately Mary's phone rang. It was T.

"So, it's our new way to keep information all together. I guess all the daily sales and calendars will be there, and any other important information. We also have access to files from corporate. Make sure you click on the welcome email, so you have access."

"Seriously T. This is so dumb. What is wrong with the old way of getting information? I can't keep up with all of these changes."

"I know, right? Let's see how long it lasts, or if it even works. Are we on for lunch today?"

"Definitely, let's go to Pingüino upstairs though. I've heard the food is better now that Chef is gone."

"Ok, see you later."

Mary hung up the phone, she hit accept on Groupies email, then got up and went to the sales floor. Olga came running up to her as she was walking through the Gifts & Home department.

"Mary, I have Oblinsky and this new customer, Penkins, at same time!" Olga always seemed out of breathe, running about like everything was an emergency. Her broken English and Russian accent were hard to understand. "One needs chinchilla, other drum."

"Sorry Olga, did you say drum?"

"Yes, drum. Fly in air for son, gift."

"Drums that fly. I, uh, don't think we carry anything like that."

"Yes, yes, on sale. In tech." Olga was now waving her hands in the air like a helicopter.

Then it dawned on Mary what it was she was talking about. "Do you mean the wireless drones, that fly with cameras attached to them?"

"Yes, yes Mary. That is it. Good price, right? For boy?"

"It would be a great gift for her son. You will have to see Sam in your area for the chinchilla. Does Mrs. Oblinsky want a coat for this winter?"

"Coat for good deal you know," Olga replied as she walked on towards the tech department.

Now that that matter was taken care of, Mary was observing the sales staff in the area. Half of the associates were assisting customers — thankfully, there were some - and the other half had their heads down, immersed in their phones. Shaking her head, Mary strolled over to the escalator. She often gazed at the enormous aquarium that rose between the sparkly winding escalators. A school of exotic fish swam by. So peaceful. If only Mary felt this calm all the time at the HeidtMoore. She was grateful for working where she did in the store. The fourth floor was the best view as you could see the entire tank from top to bottom, as it was in the middle of the store.

Mary looked over the holiday garland draped meticulously around the tank. *Pietro really is talented.* Inside the tank, he had even placed holiday accents within the coral and algae covered rocks. It was magical.

Ping. Ping.

Her smart watch startled her. She really needed to fix her notifications.

GAG GROUPIES.

The message was from T. *What on earth could that mean?* Mary quickly went back to her office to call T.

"T, why are you gagging. I thought you liked this new feature?"

"Mary, this is ridiculous. Gag! I hate Groupies. I added some of the sales data from last years 'Hot Chocolate' event. You know it's our biggest two hours of the entire year, and well, now I can't find it. Fucking ridiculous."

"Calm down, T. You know it has to be there. A file doesn't just disappear. Hold on," Mary proceeded to log onto her Groupies icon on her desktop. "I will log on and check."

"I added it under HeidtMoore Last Year Event file. Now that file is nowhere to be seen."

"Um let's see. I see HM," browsing down the lists of file folders. "You are right. No events. How about under the one that says Corporate buying office?"

"Mary, why on earth would a store event be under the buying tab?" T replied with a sarcastic questionable voice. "For fuck's sake, how the hell did it get there!?" T exclaimed as she spotted the file. "I tell you Mary this Groupies thing is not going to work. Too many places and ways to lose things."

"Well, hopefully I won't have to be on it much. I'm just now figuring out how I-Snoop works. Let me know when you mastered this Groupies

109

and then I will try. I have to go, but I'll see you at one o'clock upstairs. This day better go fast!"

"See you then," said T and hung up the phone and then resumed her work on the files. The sales numbers and other data from events was serious business. Mr. Heidt had always been a stickler for data, and correct data. Everything needed to be very accurate. T had been allowed some flexibility in the last few months since he had not been there. Boggs and Sloan didn't really care too much. But now that Mr. Heidt was back, albeit a different capacity, T was proactive in getting him the results from last years' event.

As T was teaching herself Groupies, Pietro came running in the office. "Shit T, the reindeer are here, and Antonio hasn't made space in the basement. Where is Sloan?"

"I'm not his babysitter Pietro. You have a phone."

"Eww, what's with you?"

"Groupies."

"Who?"

"You haven't read your email today have you?"

"T, I have the front window installation. Reindeers. Hot Chocolate wonderland," giving the word extra emphasis. "No time for the 100 emails a day we receive."

"Well you better get on Groupies. Evidently that is where all the files are going, including your visual masterpieces."

Just then Vivian walked in, "Pietro your reindeers are in the parking lot. You better handle that before Nacho sees."

"Viv, I know. I have to find Sloan. Have you seen him?"

"No, but I came up the freight through the back. You know he is probably on the floor."

Waving his arms in the air dramatically, Pietro left the office mumbling something.

"So dramatic," Viv said, walking into her office and shutting the door.

The entire day was filled with people entering and exiting the executive office looking for someone or something. T found it humorous that the life around her was closely resembling her lost files on Groupies. By the time 5 o'clock rolled around she was more than ready to be done for the day. She grabbed her iPad, her laptop, her iPhone, and her earbuds and headed for the door.

LET'S DRINK

Mary had survived the final holiday set up and was in desperate need of a margarita. She was exhausted, but a happy hour at Flirty Birds would do just the trick.

"Are you ready?" Mary texted T. Watching the bubble box on her phone, waiting for the reply, she gathered her handbag and bottled water and headed to the freight elevator.

"Meet you in LP." T replied.

Just a block away was the local hang out for all the managers who worked at the HeidtMoore. Flirty Birds was a bar and restaurant that just happened to offer a 30% discount to HeidtMoore employees. Mary was never much of a drinker as she suffered from lock jaw if she had cheap alcohol. Actually, any alcohol would put her jaw in a tight lock. It was something to do with the tannins that caused an excruciating pain in her jaw. Over the summer however, Mary and T frequented the bar so often that she knew one drink would be fine. The mango margarita with Tajin salt was her absolute favorite.

T and Mary got a seat at the bar. Mary was dressed in an expensive red and pink floral Dolce & Gabana dress, cut beautifully. T dressed in a Lafayette blouse and Stella McCartney pencil skirt. They definitely were the best dressed people in the room.

T looked approvingly at what Mary was wearing.

"Love." This simple exclamation was all that was needed amongst the many who worked in retail. With so little said, it meant so much.

"Thank you! Got it last season at the Consolidation sale. I thought it was kind of multi-seasonal, right?"

"Oh very! Can't believe you wore it and your high heels for holiday set up."

"No, I had to wear an elf outfit for that! Believe me, I couldn't wait to put this on afterwards."

"Hey! watch my drink." exclaimed Mary, as several pieces of glitter flew off Mary and sprinkled across the table.

"T, I just can't with the glitter. It's fucking everywhere." More glitter flew off, just missing T's martini. "And this Dolce is ruined."

"Mary, you're being a bit dramatic. Your Dolce is just fine. Have a drink. Relax." T said scanning the bar to see who was around.

"You're right. So, are you ready for your race?", taking a sip of her margarita.

"Yes, just two more weeks to go. I can't believe I'm doing a full marathon!" T gulped her drink down.

"You'll do great. I can't even make it 5 miles! Speaking of Nacho wants to run again tomorrow morning." Then Mary took a sip of her margarita.

"True love. Do it. It's not like you have Mr. Heidt barking orders at you. Come in a little late if you need to. I mean most department stores *have* a general manager. We don't. I mean, Boggs and Sloan do not count as much as they try to outdo one another and act like they own the store."

"Mr. Heidt. What a mystery. So, have you decided if you are going to keep working for him?"

"Working for him? That's been over a year. I don't think he'll be coming back now. Not after everything that's happened. He will just keep taking his calls remotely. And between us, half the time I don't think it's even him on the call." T motioned for another drink from the bartender.

"Nice life! He's emailing a lot too. I get maybe five a day. So strange." Mary was not entirely sure how someone could keep working when they were never seen. A sighting at the Commitments resort didn't count!

The bartender brought the ladies another round of drinks.

"Guess what else happened today?" asked T, finishing one drink, and going on to her second margarita.

"Olga sold you something you didn't even know you wanted," Mary replied sarcastically, feeling the material of her dress.

"Brandi called out for the third day in a row."

"That's not good. Who is in charge of Human Resources? It's a shitshow. Half of my employees have had their commission statements wrong."

"I know. It's a real mess. Then there's the business with Chef."

"Has she stopped crying over Chef? Please tell me she has! I'm so glad she let him go. What a player!"

"Yeah, I don't think she's doing too well. Hope the few days will let her get her act together. Without a functioning HR department, this holiday season is going to be BAD."

"I know, don't say that. I feel like I've got lock jaw coming on!" Mary said in mock horror.

"She did tell me something interesting..."

"Oh?"

"Oh yes, she told me about a secret room in the HeidtMoore! We need to find it!"

"A secret room? What? Do tell."

"Here's the thing. She can't remember where she saw it."

"Typical."

"But Brandi said it was filled with old merchandise. Stacked floor to ceiling. I mean, we're talking vintage Dior, Chanel, dresses, coats, handbags – you name it!" Then after a moment, T asked, "Do you think I should ask Mr. Heidt about it?"

"Maybe, but he's been gone for so long, you think he'd even remember?"

"Good point."

"But now I'm so curious. Where is this room?" Mary asked as she hiccupped. "I think we should go find it."

"Mary, hiccups are a sign you are getting tipsy," T said laughing at her. "I want to find the room too, let's pay and go check it out. We have time before the store closes."

The girls paid their tab and left Flirty Birds. Walking the short block back to the store they had time to discuss a game plan. Passing employees who were leaving for the night, it was obvious they were going in the wrong direction. Mary felt it necessary to speak to each person they passed to tell them that she and T were just going back to the store to get the handbag she had left in her office. A complete fib, but it seemed to work!

Upon entering the employee entrance, they ran into Brad who was the lead loss prevention investigator. He worked for Nacho and had been reprimanded several times by Nacho for not taking his job more seriously.

"Um, ladies you know the store closes in 15 minutes." Brad said trying to act authoritatively.

T replied, "Hey Brad, you're so great." She said placating him. "You know I just forgot to grab my iPad and I know Mr. Heidt will be sending me stuff later tonight. I just need to run up." Knowing Brad would be watching from the 30 plus security cameras she beat him to the punch. "Do you mind just watching, you know, I get creeped out when the lights are out."

"I got you T. Don't worry."

The girls quickly walked down the hall to the freight elevator. The plan was for Mary to explore the back halls of floors two through four, and T was going up to the executive office on floor six, then to check the hallways on that floor and the Fine Five. All within fifteen minutes. They would need to move swiftly if they were going to accomplish the task at hand.

Mary exited the elevator on floor two and walked quickly down the hallway, trying the door codes on each door. All of them opened and nothing was out of the ordinary, or something she had not already seen. *I'm glad to see these stock rooms are shit-show, like my areas. I need to get my area cleaned up soon.*

T exited the elevator on floor six and began to try the door codes on each door down the dark hallway. It was completely dark, so she used her phone flashlight to find her way. As she neared the last door before the stairwell, she saw a silhouette. "Who's there?" T whispered, as she walked closer.

"I thought you were going to your office?"

It was Brad.

"Fuck Brad! You scared me to death. I was, but all of a sudden, the lights went out. I was trying to find that room full of clothes everyone has been talking about." She hoped he knew what she was referring to.

"Room full of clothes? Yeah, no. I would know if there was a secret room. I'm on the security team you know."

Exactly, T thought. Of course, he was no help. Besides Nacho, the security team was mediocre at best. They had run out of time to look any further, so she headed down the stairs back to LP to meet Mary.

Once the girls were out of the store, they shared that neither of them had found anything. While they were busy playing detectives, they had missed the emails from Boggs stating the return of Mr. Heidt to the store.

The email read:

Back in time for our big surprise collaboration, Mr. Heidt will be giving his first interview in two years with Linda Langley and celebrating our biggest sales event of the year. Managers, start getting ready!

PROOF IS IN THE PROFILE

A few days later T was sitting at her desk in the executive office, scrolling down her phone, when Mary came in holding two giant canisters of petit fours.

"Hey, T. How's it going? Boggs in? I need him to check if these are out or if we need to take them off the floor," gesturing towards the canisters. "We just got a complaint that they aren't cooked. Pretty incredible if that's true. Although it kind of doesn't surprise me." But T wasn't responding. "I just don't want to have to pull 8000 units from the shelves." Still no response. "Oh, why is 'holiday' so painful...?"

T said nothing. Instead she was immersed in her phone.

Mary knocked on the table to get her attention.

"Hello? T?"

At last, T took her eyes off her phone. "Sorry, I've been...I've been setting up my online profile."

"Oh? How's it going? I've heard a lot of people are very successful on dating apps." Mary said, being polite, but really wanting to resolve the canister issue and satisfy the customer.

"What do you think of this," T proceeded to read what was on her dating profile. "Hi, my name is T. I'm 35. I love animals and the occasional glass of wine. I- "

Mary couldn't believe what she was hearing.

"Whoa, whoa, whoa…first of all you are forty-five, not thirty-five. And you told me you've never owned an animal."

"That doesn't mean I don't like them!" T said protesting.

"And you drink every night."

"Not *every* night. Just most nights and anyway, it's only a glass, or two."

"The only thing that is true is that your name is T."

T looked hurt by the accusations.

"But it's not lying…It's just exaggerating the truth…a bit. That's all. You don't know how hard it is. Trying to meet people. It's awful. I don't want to end up alone."

"You won't. You'll find someone. You will. Don't worry." Mary really had no time for a pity party. "Listen, I do need to find Boggs. Is he in?"

T's mind was not on work. "It's okay for you to say. You've got your whole life ahead of you. Me? I've got nothing. I'll probably still be single, and still be working here when I'm eighty years old and using a cane to get around the executive office." She said dramatically, as if the previous two marriages had never happened.

"You think the company will last that long?" Mary couldn't resist.

T frowned. Then suddenly distracted by a ping from her phone, T looked down to see the new dating app message that had arrived.

Her excitement quickly turned to disappointment. T read the message aloud to Mary.

"Ugh! Listen to this: *Hi there beautiful. You're a catch and I've got my line out.*"

T looked up at Mary.

"Seriously? Is he for real? This is so depressing. I'm never going to meet anyone. Anyone! These are the jerks who are out there. Unbelievable."

"Don't be down. Come to Flirty Birds tonight after work. I'll be there, Nacho, Sarafina…That's if I can resolve this issue."

"Maybe. Oh, look at this one…this one is a CEO, he's handsome, went to Yale…"

"See? It's not all doom and gloom. Now I really need to deal with this issue, where is Boggs?"

"I don't know. Check the back."

Mary walked through to the back of the executive office, but no sign of Boggs. Walking back Mary said her goodbye to T, reiterated the invitation to meet after work, and went on her way to find Boggs.

An hour later, she found Boggs in the Ladies Shoes department straightening Jimmy Choos.

"Thank goodness I found you. We have an issue."

"What is it?"

"These canisters." Mary explained the whole issue to Boggs about how they hadn't been cooked and how the customer was threatening to sue unless she got a 30% discount on all items for life.

"Well, first things first, let's do a taste test." He said opening up one of the canisters. Boggs took off the wrapping and opened the tin. Taking out one of the delicacies, he put one in his mouth and offered one to Mary. "Mmmn…Not bad. A bit chewy maybe."

"I mean, do you think we need to remove them?"

"Yes, take them down. The customer says they are bad. We take em' down."

"But it does say here on the canister that that they are meant to be chewy and doughy. How can we be sure that these are undercooked?"

"Customer is always right."

"We are going to lose so much in sales. This is our number one best seller and we've been selling them fine so far." Mary really did not want to give up her inventory. If she removed these canisters she would have to somehow make up the loss. Then it would be virtually impossible to do the sort of sales figures needed to make the season.

"But it was just this one customer." But his mind was made up. Mary spent the rest of the day unloading canisters off the floor.

At around 6:30 p.m., T texted Mary. "Thanks for the invite for tonight. But I have a date. Super excited! Thanx for advice."

Meanwhile at Flirty Birds, Sarafina, Nacho and a few others were having drinks waiting for Mary to arrive. The bar was busy and packed with the locals, consisting mainly of people who worked at the HeidtMoore. The sales associates came to unwind after a grueling day at work. It was the perfect spot for after work drinks and the bartenders knew mostly everyone by name.

"Where's Mary tonight?" inquired Sean, a friendly young bartender at Flirty Birds.

"Good question. She should be here. We were meant to meet here," said Nacho, trying to keep his cool. He was really looking forward to seeing Mary. Not that he would ever let her know that it was the one thing in the workday that kept him going. "Well, I guess I'll take another one." Sean poured Nacho another Jack and Coke.

It was 8:30 p.m. and back at the store, Mary was still dealing with the canisters. She had completely forgotten about the happy hour as she was so intently working on completely the job. She had a long night ahead of her. As there were thirty more canisters to take off the floor, and remove from inventory, and then fill in the missing spaces on the shelves with new stock.

Mary texted Nacho, two hours after they were supposed to meet. "Nacho, I am so so sorry I missed tonight! I am dealing with inventory issues." She felt awful about standing him up. But work came first. At least for the time being.

DATE NIGHT FRIGHT NIGHT

T was on the latest dating app, *On the Rocks*, an app especially designed for divorcées since she was twice divorced. She was having just as much luck as Sloan was trying to find true love using his dating app.

"How did your date go last night?" asked Mary the following day, during the startup meeting.

"Don't ask."

"That bad huh?"

"Not good. He was an hour late. Then he asked me to pick up the check at the end of dinner. But you know what? Today is a new day. I will not give up."

"Good. Don't!"

Sloan interrupted the girls chatting in the back of the room.

"Perhaps you would like to share your important news? There seems to be a lot of talk going on back there." Everyone was silent and Mary was feeling like she was back in school. "Interesting. Well, then perhaps you would like to share your sales numbers from yesterday with me."

T took her lunch at the usual time of 1:00 p.m. She typically ate in the employee breakroom if she wasn't having lunch with Mary in the

Pingüino. It was a small room that was once two dressing rooms. The management team had converted the space into a spot for associates to take their breaks.

Ting Ting. T's dating app notification went off.

She glanced down at her phone.

Pending match. Cocktails anyone? Reply now!

T opened the message and was pleased she did.

A handsome face appeared. He was just T's kind of guy. He was tall, dark, and handsome and a CEO. His name was Tom. Reading his profile, she said "yes" to meeting up. T was so tired. Tired of dating, tired of getting married and divorced and just simply tired. She couldn't for some reason find a man that was, in her mind, decent.

Husband number one had run off with her late father's inheritance. It was then that she was forced to get a job and she landed in retail. Actually, when she first started at the HeidtMoore she loved it; the forty five percent discount, helping customers and assisting Mr. Heidt. This was before Mr. Heidt started spending long periods of time away from the store. With his prolonged absences she felt she was taking on double, if not triple the work, and without the proper pay. Then, there was husband number two, who fell in love with his shrink. T simply had terrible luck with men.

A week later she decided to meet the "On the Rocks" man at a Mexican restaurant. This was a well-known Mexican restaurant in Dallas and T loved going there. This would be a safe place to meet someone on a first date.

T walked through the doors to the restaurant and was greeted by the hostess.

"Hola, señorita T," said the hostess handing her a menu. T pondered the fact that the hostess knew her name, then T realized she was wearing her name badge from work.

"Oh, ha. Oops. Gotta take off my name," said T, unlinking her HeidtMoore name badge, and slipping it into her pocket. "I'm here to meet a friend. Just going to the bar." T gave back the menu and walked to the bar. She didn't see Tom, but she did see…the tech trainer from work! *Adam? What was he doing here?*

"Hey. I'm Tom. Are you T97?"

"Yes, but isn't your real name Adam?"

"Yeah, Hey, Wait. You work at the HeidtMoore right?"

"I do, yes. But why did you put a picture of someone else on your profile? And why is your name Tom?" T did not feel comfortable. Something was seriously off.

"Oh that." Blowing it off like it was nothing. "You can't be too careful these days. Last month I had a date and the person kept being such a psycho. I was stalked, quite literally."

T couldn't argue with that. She'd had some scary experiences herself.

"I know. Me too. Like last week I had a date with a guy that made me pay for everything and then asked me to meet his mom. So weird." Then realizing she may have given too much information out. "Sorry. I probably shouldn't have said that."

"No, no I love to hear you talk. Continue." What the heck. T was here now. She may as well stay. Who knows? Maybe this would lead somewhere? It was a good thing she did stay. The evening turned out to be very enjoyable. The pair stayed until closing and they found out they both had lots in common, as both worked in the retail world.

T told him about her failed marriages and her time at the HeidtMoore, and he told her all about the new app he was introducing and how he became a tech expert. T was suitably impressed. He had studied at Texas Tech and, like T, had also been married before. It was a sad story. He told T that his ex-wife had run off with someone. That someone was his best friend. Awkward!

Before the night had ended Adam had kissed T. It was 11:00 p.m. and they had polished off four margaritas each and were feeling no pain. T contemplated whether she should follow him for a night cap.

"Come on, let's go. One more."

"I don't know. I have an early start tomorrow. I cannot be hungover. Cannot." T was trying to be firm in both thought and stature.

Adam looked back at her with pleading eyes.

She couldn't resist. "Oh, ok. Just one."

T got home at 3am, a little worse for wear.

The following day was a struggle! First, T overslept and did not hear her alarm. Then when she did get to the store, she was inundated with tech requests and demands from both Sloan and Boggs.

"You're a little late this morning," said Sloan looking at his watch.

"I had a date. It went well but…yes, perhaps a cup of black coffee wouldn't go amiss."

"A date? With whom? Do tell!" T couldn't tell if Sloan really wanted to know, or if he was just jealous that she actually had gone on a date.

"It was good. Nice guy." She said coyly, pouring herself a cup of black coffee. "Okay, you want to know who it is? The tech trainer! Adam!"

"The techie!" Sloan shrieked. "Seriously? I thought he bats for the other team."

"Oh no. No, he certainly does not." T said with a smile across her face. "I kind of feel good about this one. We'll see. But what's going on with you? Any luck?"

"Are you kidding me? Nothing. Everyone online, they are just so eeww, gross. But I am happy for you. That's great." Then moving the subject to business, Sloan handed T a financial report he had. "So, let's talk about this report. I need TY numbers against LY and so far, you have only given me TY."

SLOAN'S IDEA FOR XMAS

Sloan, always wanting to compete with Boggs, was feeling insecure about the Go Green collaboration with CJ Nickels. He knew he had to think of something quick. Something bigger! Something better!

The idea came to him one evening while at home. Perusing dating apps. If T could find love, so could he. He was looking through *On the Rocks*, which was too straight for him, *JDate*, no cute men, *Grindon*, too promiscuous, and *gayharmony*, which was too gay. He was wishing there were an app that could create the perfect man for him.

Sloan's mind wandered to the beauty bots.

The "ladies" of beauty were dominating the sales floor. The robots' ability to provide perfect makeovers, to endlessly listen to customers and to giving affirmations. Of course, employee perfection had proven to be a success. The "ladies" never arrived late, never called in sick or never quit the job unexpectedly, as so many beauty associates often did. Unless they were not re-charged each night, they worked seamlessly. Then Sloan had his Eureka moment.

That's it! A DIGITAL DYNASTY!!

Sloan emailed his cousin, Hayley Moore in the buying office, immediately.

Hi Hayley,

How fast can we get the new tech items for the fourth floor? Christmas is coming early this year to the HeidtMoore and we must be ready! I want to add a gift component with tech and really blast out the floor. Create a virtual experience for our customers in every way. Let's Face Time tomorrow!

Sloan felt certain this idea would propel him to the top. All he needed was about ten or so super tech, high powered, items to sell over the holidays and *boom!* It promised to be an instant success! How could cheap recycled products compete with the latest technological gadgets?

Peanut approached his master with his ball. Taking it from Peanut's mouth, Sloan threw the ball across the room. It accidentally smashed into the glass sliding door and luckily bounded off. However, it managed to hit the iPad on a side table by the door and broke the glass screen. Overlooking this mishap, Sloan laughed, as Peanut wagged his tail with the ball in his mouth begging for another throw.

"Oh Peanut, what are we going to do with you?" Despite cracking his iPad screen, Sloan couldn't get mad at his dog, with those sad puppy eyes.

Sloan got back online and continued scrolling through dating apps. He was bound to find the perfect man. Now that everything was going his way. Minutes later his stomach was growling. Unlike Boggs who enjoyed staying in shape, Sloan despised a workout. He thought eating healthier would be a way to slim down. He picked up his phone and tapped on his latest restaurant app "My Pho-King Dumplings."

My Pho-King Dumplings was the newest Thai restaurant in Uptown and was a favorite of Sloan's. He had his order saved to "favorites" on the app, so it only took a moment to place. Just as he finished, he received a reply back from Hayley.

Cousin,

Fabulous idea! I was just in a meeting today discussing the store and added features for this Christmas. Attached is a list of some gift ideas from market that I know you will love. Look through and let me know what quantities needed. Lunch soon?

Sloan knew Hayley would be the right person to contact for his idea and he was right. The attachment had a list of gifts that were exactly what he had in mind for his Digital Dynasty. His mind raced to get back to the store in the morning to plan out the floor layout. Before leaving to get his dinner from Pho-King Dumplings, he sent a quick text to Mary. To Sloan, it didn't matter what time of day or night it was, he never restrained from contacting any of the employees. So, he texted Mary at 8:30 p.m. on a Tuesday night.

Mary,

We are doing a floor move in Tech end of week. Make sure you have associates scheduled to help.

Mary just happened to have her phone near and saw the text. Sloan had a bad habit of just texting at all hours as if every manager were "on call." She didn't help to discourage this behavior as she always replied immediately. "Got it, I will have plenty of staff there."

As soon as Sloan returned from the restaurant with his dumplings and spring rolls, he sat down at his dining room table. He checked the text reply from Mary and was pleased. He knew he could count on Mary. She had really proven herself during the spring Hudson Hawn runway presentation. Furthermore, she had shown great leadership and accountability with the holiday installation.

Reviewing the pages and pages of merchandise suggestions Hayley had sent over, Sloan scrolled through each between bites of dumplings, splattering soy sauce on his laptop.

Hours later he had selected what he thought would be the best merchandise for the holiday season. He hoped to ramp up the sales and prove he was the best choice for general manger if Mr. Heidt did not return to the store in full capacity. Sloan also selected his next weeks' order from Sakara Life for his lunches. He was determined to lose a few pounds before Christmas!

Hoping Hayley would still be up and would check her phone he sent her his list along with some incredibly detailed notes about his idea for the floor. He envisioned a stainless-steel ultra-modern pop-up display in the tech area of the fourth floor. Upon entering, customers would be able to see, touch, and listen to each item before purchasing. There would be a professional expert at each station to show clients how each gadget worked and could be customized to their liking. The associates would wear a fitted Prada lab coat and coordinating Tom Ford spectacles to "look smart" and stand out. The team would have special earpieces and hidden microphones so client questions and information could be shared without the customer knowing. Then as the customer tried each tech item it would appear the associates knew what they wanted before the customer did. By the time the customer had finished the exhibition the items would be wrapped and ready at the POS station at the end of the aisle. Sloan thought the entire idea as really quite futuristic and "out of the box" thinking at its finest! A real genius lab! A HeidtMoore first. *A Digital Dynasty!*

The only problem he could think of was how to get more associates. In the past he would have gone to the HR Manager, Frank, and just asked to hire additional holiday help. He knew this year would be different since Frank was retired. Brandi was no use. Maybe she just would be. Sloan jotted off an email to Brandi,

Brandi, I need 8 smart associates hired for holiday. They need to be in the next training class and look good in glasses. Let's chat tomorrow after the start up.

Pressing send he closed his laptop, pleased with his progress. He looked over at Peanut, who had been sleeping peacefully on the couch. Peanut sat up and gave a low bark as if to "agree" with Sloan, then laid back down. Sloan moved to the couch and sat beside Peanut opening up his phone app to see if there were any new messages from any of the dating apps. One message on *gayharmony*:

Looking for love, must love to hike and workout.

Glad he had the next day's workload ahead to keep his mind off being single, Sloan headed for bed.

INITIATIVE OVERLOAD—GO GREEN OR GO DIGITAL

It was now late October, and the store was heaving twinkle lights and mistletoe. Forget Halloween, forget Thanksgiving! In typical HeidtMoore form the store did do an outpost for Columbus Day!

Mary was knee deep in holiday. Not only was she responsible for Boggs's *Go Green* with CJNickels collaboration, but she also now had to juggle Sloan's brand-new *Digital Dynasty* initiative that had been announced a few days prior. Mary had to set up the '*Happy HeidtMoore Holiday Shop*'. And it wasn't even November.

The question on every manager's mind was, which one of the two acting general managers would outperform the other? With two initiatives, each with their own massive sales goals, and two micromanaging bosses, Boggs and Sloan, the season was feeling very hectic indeed.

A notification came across Mary's Apple Watch. Secretly hoping it was Nacho, she glanced down to read the message.

We have another shipment of Holiday in receiving. Where to put?? The text was from Willie.

Just unload by the freight elevator and we will get to it eventually. Mary replied back using the microphone on the watch.

Fortunately, Mary had the holiday help she needed. She managed to convince both Boggs and Sloan that four of the Beauty Bots would be useful in her department. They proved to be amazingly helpful unpacking the boxes of tech gifts and the beauty associates were very pleased they were off the floor in their department. Mary found the products quite entertaining and wondered how they would sell. Sloan's idea could really take off.

Some of the *Digital Dynasty* items were:

Bye Frownisha—a gadget to remove the "eleven" lines between your brows.

Hey Babe—the latest smart speaker, better than Alexa, Siri, or Google with the ability to personalize the voice to your real-life partner

HyperPlay—fit bit for children.

Bilingual Barker—a collar that translates what pets are really yapping about.

Later that same afternoon, Mary received a shipment of the *Go Green* items. Interestingly, Boggs had managed to bring in items that combined green elements WITH tech. She would have loved to see the look on Sloan's face when Boggs announced his products. That's if he had said anything in the first place.

Some of the *Go Green* items were:

Marry Me Juana—a weed plant that produced leaves suitable for afternoon tea.

21 day-no tox-briefs—for men, who do not like to do laundry

Rehydrating vodka—a special formulation that rehydrates your system and provides a buzz when needed

The Emperor Clothing App—purchase this advanced app that literally dresses you from head to toe. But be careful if you are in a 'no service' phone zone! When your phone is fully connected your outfit can change with just a swipe.

The 'Go Green for 5 cents' - Mary's nickname for all the cheap crap coming into the luxurious department store - merchandise was unboxed by the five Bots. Even though most of the holiday splendor was located on Mary's fourth floor, the executives had decided to expand to multiple levels. The merchandise was placed neatly on metal bakers racks, waiting to be displayed in the set up around the escalators on the Handbag and Jewelry level.

Gone were the days of additional Visual help with merchandise and overseeing the visuals for the store. Back when Mr. Heidt Sr. started the HeidtMoore there were visual teams on each level of the department store. Now it was down to just Pietro and his small team, one person for each level of the large department store.

Always finding herself offering to do more than her job required, Mary proceeded to roll a loaded rack of *Go Green* merchandise onto the freight elevator.

Mary sent a quick text to Pietro.

We have more 5-cent merch, I'm taking it down and putting it out. Have one of your guys look at it in the morning and tweak if needed.

The freight elevator finally arrived after taking forever to open. Walking out of the freight elevator was T pushing a merchandise cart packed with office supplies.

"Good God, you look like you purchased all of Staples."

"Tell me about it!"

"How is it going with Adam?"

"Great! We Face Timed for four hours last night."

"That's a long FaceTime. He lives in the city, right?" Mary was a little perplexed as to why they didn't meet in person.

"It's what we do. We Face Time and text. Gotta go. See you later."

Mary wheeled the loaded rack onto the already full freight. *Typical* she thought. *Why does everyone think the freight is where rolling rods should be stored?* It drove Mary nuts.

Shoving the rods aside, she managed to squeeze in the rack along with pulling a thread in her new Balmain silk knit double-breasted jacket. "Damn it!"

Mary made room on nearly every shelf. Along the escalator for the new 5 cent goods. It took three times as long as needed, because she kept getting distracted by the epicure items. Known for her sweet tooth, Mary couldn't help but pick up and examine each box of chocolate, caramels, and candy-coated delights. Since working for HeidtMoore, Mary had gained nearly fifteen pounds and blamed it all on the Epicure department. Every day they had samples of new items along with the famous HeidtMoore classics. Mary was a regular visitor, and her waistline was proof. It was some motivation to keep running with Nacho. Luckily, he had never made any comments.

As she was nearly finished, her phone buzzed with a reply from Pietro. "Will do. Just put the extra stuff in the room next to the freight on 3."

Once Mary had finished merchandising the floor, she rolled the bakers racks with remaining items to the back hall and looked for the room Pietro had requested. She entered the code to the door just to the right of the elevator. Looking for the light switch she took out her phone and turned on the flashlight. The room was small with a few bars for hanging clothes on one side and a curtain draped across on the opposite side. Upon opening it she was in shock. It was the secret room! Why hadn't she seen this before? Mary could not wait to tell T.

She was already into overtime and late for her date with Nacho. Instead of taking the remaining empty racks down to the basement, where they belonged, she left them in the freight elevator, and did not think twice about doing so.

PANDY GETS PAMPERED

Zane, one of the top producers in beauty and in the whole store, was prepping for an appointment with a new client. His 'home base' bay as it was called, was where he usually took all of his appointment requests, but this new client would take him out of his comfort zone and into all new areas. By 'new areas', it meant another department of the store.

When the HeidtMoore first opened, associates were hired to sell from only one area. They were specialized in everything to do with that particular product assortment. Zane had that home base mentality. He knew his product like a sommelier knows wine. But anything outside of his bay was a whole new world. In keeping with the times, Mr. Heidt Jr. had instructed Boggs and Sloan to make sure all associates could now sell all over the store. This was quite a different mentality than what had been instilled in him for years.

It was an interesting dynamic for Mary to watch the old school specialists and the new school stylists compete for the same customer.

Zane was to meet Mr. Pandy Penkins in the Mens department on the third floor. Sloan had referred him to Zane, after the conversation he had with Mr. Penkins about nuts, in the Epicure department. Mr. Penkins, short in stature and plump, reminded Zane of the Monopoly board game man, with his little round glasses and piercing blue eyes and top hat. This would be Zane's first time working with him and even though he wasn't comfortable leaving his zone to assist him, he was banking on a fat commission from whatever it was he would sell to Mr. Penkins.

Promptly at 3 p.m., Mr. Penkins pulled up to the valet door in his vintage gold Rolls Royce, and then made his way up to the third floor. Zane was there to meet him. Even though it was such a burden for Zane to have to leave his coveted cosmetics floor to go to floor 3 he knew deep down it would be worth the dividends.

"Welcome to the HeidtMoore Mr. Penkins! What a lovely day we are going to have! We are so happy to see you," Zane announced.

"Great, great, no fuss, please. Just need a suit for this holiday. Not a lot of time," Mr. Penkins replied.

"Of course, let's get started. Are we thinking plaid or pinstripe?" Zane led Mr. Penkins to the Brioni area.

Noticing the snake eyes from the other tenured employees, Zane knew what they all were thinking. *Why is Zane in this area, he doesn't know a thing about suits?* Partly true, but Zane did have one thing—style.

Hoping Mr. Penkins was open to his taste in fashion, Zane was excited about the opportunity to sell a $10,000 sport coat. *Why not?* Zane had nothing to lose. He knew he could probably sell even more. Zane had done his homework and looped in the Mens manager to assist him, who had set up a fitting room with different options and swatch books.

Mr. Pandy Penkins was pleasantly surprised with the atmosphere. Comfy couches, several mirrors, a fully stocked bar cart, and a tv that took up an entire wall.

"Well this is really nice, the only thing missing is some fruit and nuts," said Mr. Penkins.

As if on cue, Vivian, the HeidtMoore Public Relations Manager, rolled another cart into the room filled with items from 'Pandy's Nuts from Lubbock'. One thing the HeidtMoore knew how to do was to entertain a guest. It was what the Heidts' prided themselves on – amazing customer service! From custom horse-riding crops, to an evening at the

Pingüino with personalized place settings, the HeidtMoore knew how to engage and flatter anyone and everyone.

Sloan was next to enter the fitting room scene. It was a long traditions for one or both of the assistant general managers to greet top customers, offering the added touch of personal service. Before knocking on the door, Sloan scanned the area and realized the potential, having Mr. Penkins engaged in shopping. He instantly sent a group text to all the managers in the store.

Alert! Opulence in the building. We need to surprise and delight in Mens. I expect each of you to make a personal appearance.

This was a text message that every manager knew meant opportunity for their area. Every working manager pretty much dropped what they were doing and grabbed their favorite items from the HeidtMoore and took them down to the Mens area. They each pulled Zane aside and gave him a quick tutorial on their products and how they should be presented to this high net worth client.

Four hours later, Zane rang $50,000 in suiting, $25,000 in women's apparel, jewelry, shoes and handbags, and another $3000 in face care products.

The next day, when he arrived for work, Zane saw on the sales board he had made number one on the list of top sellers! *Nice!* That was two months' worth of rent he didn't need to worry about now.

TEVI'S RETURN TO THE ZOO

After two months away from the HeidtMoore, Tevi returned. This was just in time for the wild energy brought on by the holidays. This holiday was going to be fierce and not in a good way.

The busiest time for any retail store was November and December, and the HeidtMoore was no different. Tevi was anxious to see how the store looked "all dressed up." She had received some updates from Mary while she was at Commitments, but had trouble downloading the pictures Mary was sending her. Despite being so cutting edge, Commitments didn't have the best Wi-Fi. To get the full experience, Tevi was going to break normal protocol and enter through the main entrance. She wanted to see the store from the clients' perspective. Hoping Nacho and Brad were too busy to notice, she walked right through the gold doors at eleven o'clock.

Upon entering the store, she noticed the massive holiday window display. It was a Dallas tradition that for generations the HeidtMoore holiday window meant it was time to shop! This year's window did not disappoint. Pietro had designed a wonderland, complete with a forest of "Christmas" animals that included an arctic fox, snowy owl, and puffins. The foxes' cave was made to look like a chocolate candy bar. The snowy owl sat on an enormous candy cane and the puffins drank "hot chocolate" from their perches. It was a wild, exotic sight to behold! Tevi, along with several customers paused to watch in awe at the animals and admire the window.

Suddenly ABBI approached the group.

"May I interest you in one of our La Mer spas today?" The bot asked the group, then waited for the customers to answer. To Tevi's amazement, one customer did respond.

"Yes, I'm here for the eleven o'clock with Ta'Keisha."

The bot replied, "Wonderful, Miss. Please follow me and I will show you to your spa room."

Tevi could not believe what she just witnessed. She ran as fast as her Louboutin's could take her, all the way to the escalator, anxious to find another manager who could tell her what else she had missed while she was away.

Exiting the winding escalator on the fifth floor, she ran into Sam and Hilz who were chatting in the aisle near the Dolce & Gabbana boutique area. "Welcome back Tev! Hey, did you hear about the secret room?" Sam asked Hilz.

"Yeah, no wonder our inventory has been off. Whoever has been dumping all that merchandise in there is in hot water!"

The secret room Mary had discovered was not so secret anymore. She had told T, who promptly told Brandi, who then told Trevor, a Fine Five associate, who was dating Zane, who told anyone that would listen. Mary and T had stayed late one evening to snoop through the room. As they were entering the room, they ran into Olga who was leaving as if it was nothing but a stockroom. Mary found this odd. What was even more bizarre were all the clothes and shoes they found deep in the room. Clothes from past seasons. T said they were at least 6 seasons ago. They found a huge section of custom dresses in plus sizing. The HeidtMoore carried everything but plus sizing. There was also a section with jewelry that was quite organized amongst all of the other merchandise just dumped there. It was an unbelievable sight! Mary wondered why Nacho had never mentioned this room. She left with T feeling uneasy about this secret closet.

Tevi immediately interrupted Hilz, "Oh I've known about that closet for years. It used to be where PR put all of their sample merchandise and then as we outgrew this place Willy and his team started putting returns in there. I know there aren't any handbags in there."

Hilz startled at Tevi's comment, replied, "Are you sure, because Boggs and Sloan have never mentioned it. And you would think Mr. Heidt would be all over that."

"Sha-a-yeah, if he was ever here," Sam chimed in. Before the conversation could go any further, Sloan appeared out of nowhere.

"Tevi, good to see you back. I need to update you on some changes. Let's meet in my office in 10 minutes.

"Bloody hell Sloan, I just got here."

"Right but if you have time to chat with these two," pointing to Sam and Hilz, "then you have time to chat with me. See you in a minute." He continued down the aisle.

"Why did I come back today, bloody hell," Tevi grumbled as she walked off.

Fifteen minutes later Tevi headed to the executive offices.

"T, is Sloan in his office? He wanted to update me."

"No, he left about 20 minutes ago to walk the floor."

"For fuck's sake, typical. Any idea what these updates are about?"

"Where should I start?" T threw her hands up and began telling Tevi about all the software updates to I-Snoop, Groupies, and the cloud migration. She could tell Tevi was not impressed.

"I only went by my office to grab my notebook, haven't even turned on the computer."

"Well, it probably won't work when you do. Nothing does around here lately. Well except the holiday lights."

"The front window looked bloody fantastic. Pietro really outdid himself this year."

T went on telling Tevi about Chef getting fired and how Brandi's presence at the store was becoming as infrequent as Mr. Heidt's lately.

"I knew those two had something going on. I bloody felt it. All those sweets he made." Tevi had now made herself comfortable sitting on the corner of T's desk. "Sparkle is huge. How many breakdowns has that girl had while I was away?"

The ladies continued gossiping for another 15 minutes. Lost in conversation, they both jumped when Sloan appeared at T's desk.

"Sorry Tevi, we had an issue in Cosmetics. T, call Antonio and have someone clean up by the Marc Jacobs counter. We had a lipstick catastrophe," Sloan waved his hands in the air to emphasize the dramatics of the missed situation in the beauty department. "Tevi, come on in," as he started down the hallway to his office.

LINDA LANGLEY

Linda, the famed reporter for the local news, had a new scoop. And it was big! The HeidtMoore was replacing associates with ROBOTS and s_he_ would be the one to break the news.

Known for her retail reporting, which had kept her in business for the last twenty years as a reporter, Linda's interest in the HeidtMoore department store verged on obsessive.

She was the one who broke the news on the missing general manager. She reported the news when an active shooter held managers, associates, and clients hostage. And now she would report the news about the new brand of associate, the *Robot*. Rumors had circulated for over a year that the store would be closing, but every time the store managed to keep afloat. It was some kind of miracle. Of course, it was in Linda's best interest for the store to stay open. While the store remained open, Linda was still employed.

It was 9:30 a.m. and the store was about to open. Linda was tapping on the glass door to get Boggs' attention. She smiled and waved, but no luck. Boggs didn't see her until Curious started squawking and jumping up and down. Linda was a little afraid of the diminutive monkey and hoped the animal would be put away for her interview.

As the enormous door to the store began to slide open, she was quickly greeted by Curious. *I wonder what will happen to him if these doors close permanently!*

Linda was graciously welcomed by both Boggs and Sloan. This was a pleasant surprise. She could kill two birds with one stone.

"Good morning gentleman, thank you so much for allowing our crew in to film today. They will be here momentarily. But first I thought we could talk about the Bots and Mr. Heidt." Without missing a beat and not allowing the two men to speak, she continued on. "Is it true you are replacing associates with robots?"

Both Sloan and Boggs laughed off this question.

"That's so funny. No, we're not replacing anyone with robots," said Sloan, even though there had been talk at corporate that this would make sense in the long run. Robots versus people would save so much money.

"I will have to take your word for it, I guess. But I do have my sources and my sources are often right."

"We have six robots who work in Cosmetics. And four who assist with our holiday set up. We're not getting anymore." Boggs was getting annoyed at this line of questioning. He thought Langley was here to discuss his *Go Green* Initiative.

"The holidays are here, I guess, and still no sign of Mr. Heidt." said Langley. It was more of a statement than a question.

"We are thrilled you are here and cannot wait for you to see our exclusive offerings this holiday season. Mr. Heidt will be here, as we're just confirming dates. You see, he's terribly busy," said Sloan, ushering Linda through the main floor of the Cosmetics depart.

"Is it true he's living with two Versace models, under the age of twenty, and he's undergoing rehab treatments?"

"I'm not obligated to answer that." Quickly changing the subject. "You will be the first to see our technology advances and also the importance the HeidtMoore plays in keeping our planet green."

Boggs chimed in, "also Linda since your last visit with me, we have introduced new members to the HeidtMoore family and partnered with someone I just know you will recognize."

"Gentleman, this all sounds super exciting. Where should we start?"

Both Sloan and Boggs practically jumped over each other to show the reporter just how well the HeidtMoore was doing. It was a constant race between the two of them just who could perform better.

"Let's start in cosmetics," said Sloan, before Boggs quickly jumped in.

"Actually, I was thinking we could go to Ladies Shoes first, and then the new shop we just installed upstairs on the fourth floor. You know our 'Go Green' is going to do amazingly well! We've got a lot of presell and orders already rung!" Sloan was visibly annoyed at Boggs taking the lead.

"Great. What do you think accounts for that? I mean given the fact that business in brick and mortar is trending down."

"Several things." Now it was Sloan's turn to jump in and be the retail hero. "First we have a wonderful tech initiative called 'The Digital Dynasty', I think you will just love."

"Really?"

"We offer each of our customers something digital, something curated, something personal." Sloan was on a roll, until Boggs interrupted.

"And that's why with 'Go Green' we combine tech with healthy, more nuanced options for the consumer. People don't just have to come to the HeidtMoore for the shopping, or to see the animals in the window displays, or even the world-famous fish tank. No, people also come for something special, something more mindful." Boggs said, with extra emphasis on the word *mindful*. He was always in salesman mode.

As the three of them walked through the store, there weren't many customers. It was still early but for a Friday morning this was unusual. Sales were declining and despite all of the luxury experiences the store had to offer, it felt like it wasn't enough. At this point not even the new advances in technology looked like it could save the store.

After a few hours of walking the floor, camera crew in tow, viewing the tech merchandise and the green items, Linda Langley had just what she needed to write a compelling piece. Boggs and Sloan hoped they had given her enough information about the new initiatives that she would spin a strong story and give the HeidtMoore the needed PR boost.

"Until next time gentleman, this has been a delightful morning. You know I will be back to discuss the annual Hot Chocolate event." And with that she was out the door.

VIVIAN'S EVENT

While Boggs and Sloan had been walking the store, Vivian had been busy at work on the big PR event that was going to take place. She was thrilled to hear that Linda would be in the store most of the day. This would occupy Boggs and Sloan, who would no doubt be running around like headless chickens, providing Langley with a false narrative about how the store was performing.

Linda's arrival also meant Vivian could get some work done without being interrupted by Boggs and Sloan. Or *BS* as she secretly referred to them. But first, she had a much-anticipated Skype call with Mr. Heidt. Would he really be on the call? Vivian honestly couldn't remember the last time she saw Mr. Heidt and wasn't even too sure what he looked like anymore.

An hour later she was finishing off the Skype call, without the video, with Mr. Heidt. She was one of the few people who had not upgraded to using Zoom.

"Yes sir, I think that is a great idea. We can add on to the event. The team will be happy to hear that you will be here for this event. What a way to start our holiday at the HeidtMoore! Talk soon."

Bloop.

Just like that the call had ended. He sounded like Mr. Heidt, but without seeing him, who really knew?

"T, send an email. We need to have a manager meeting after this afternoons meeting," Vivian shouted from her office into T's adjacent cubicle.

T, thankfully was in a good mood, and did not let the tone of Vivian's voice bother her, replied quickly.

"Of course, Vivian. Do we need the Ops team also or just sales managers?"

"Sales only, and T, you need to attend also."

The morning meeting had been cancelled due to the Linda Langley interview, but it didn't mean that all of the day's meetings were cancelled. Mid-afternoon, the managers met in the conference room. Boggs and Sloan had Facetimed with Mr. Heidt the previous evening and knew that Vivian could handle the meeting.

Mary was curious as to what this urgent meeting was about. Sam, the Fine Five Manager, walked to the conference room with Mary.

"Maybe we are all getting fired. You know, right before Thanksgiving."

Sarafina replied, rather mournfully, "I doubt that. They know we have Gottrocks coming for Thanksgiving."

Hilz caught up to the group, "Oh, I bet it's regarding our floor plans and the fact that we only have half the capable staff that we used to. Have you seen Brandi this morning?"

Leigha shuffling through with her notepad in hand stated, "She's here. Come on we are going to be late."

Once everyone was seated seats around the large oval desk in the conference room, Vivian began. Seated at the head of the table with Pietro at the other end, Mary knew at once that this meeting was going to be about an event.

"Ok, team. We don't have much time to pull this off," Vivian began while looking down at her yellow notepad filled with notes. "Everyone

145

knows our annual Hot Chocolate Event that happens every holiday, right? Well, this year we are expanding it." The managers all looked around at each other wondering what "expanding it" entailed.

"For starters, this year the party will be on Black Friday. And instead of just a short 2-hour event, it will be all…day…long. We are combining the launch of *Go Green* and *Digital Dynasty* with the Hot Chocolate and Black Friday."

Pietro joined in the conversation. "We have ordered 18kt. Gold cups with the HeidtMoore details. And the restaurant is preparing a special hot chocolate recipe exclusive to our store."

Vivian interrupted. "Yes, the traditions for the Hot Chocolate Event will remain. And we have partnered with the community center in Oak Cliff for an added philanthropic element. They are sending the elementary show choir for entertainment during the first hour. Mr. Heidt approved the ten percent donation from all sales made for that evening."

"That is amazing," Hilz piped in.

"Yes, the details will be handled. The important thing is for you all to get your associates on board. We must have customers to support this huge event. Mr. Nickels will be in attendance kicking off the *Be Clean Go Green* collaboration. And Mr. Heidt will do the hot chocolate toast. We need our top customers here."

Mary whispered to Nacho. "Did I hear that right? Mr. Heidt will actually be here?"

"I'll believe that when I see it," he whispered back.

Mary reverted to texting so as not to signal attention.

"Do you think he will be at the store before the event?" She quickly typed to Nacho. Glancing at his watch to read the message, he looked over to her and shrugged his shoulders. Mary looked around the room and nearly everyone was looking down at their phones. Half were frantically typing. Vivian continued discussing the event details.

"So, you see, the gold carpet will run from the front entrance down the main aisle of cosmetics to the escalator. Then again on seven, straight to Pingüino." Pietro always had the most interesting ideas.

Mary could not believe she might actually meet the store's General Manager in a few weeks! It was exciting enough that she was going to experience the Hot Chocolate Event from the inside this year, even if the whole event seemed like a chaotic nightmare. In years past, as long as she could recall, she would stand outside with her mother watching the glamorous people step inside the store for the famous Hot Chocolate Event. She always longed to do the same. To be able to step inside this glamourous store and be a part of this incredible event. Those were memories she cherished.

The annual Hot Chocolate Event was the event of the season for the HeidtMoore. It was created shortly after the store opened and had been an annual tradition ever since. Each year a different country was represented with a special hot chocolate recipe and china cup design. The store spared no expense for this evening, from invitations that included a boxed china souvenir cup, to chocolate bars and candies imported from the country represented. The front window displays were magnificent, with the animals sampling fake 'hot chocolate'. Mary had wondered since she was a child how the HeidtMoore was able to serve animals chocolate and get away with it. This would be the year she found out all the HeidtMoore secrets. Even the vendors were involved with the event. Some designers such as Michael Kors and Carolina Herrera created special pieces to be sold exclusively during the Hot Chocolate Event. Mary remembered seeing one chocolate colored silk, one shoulder ball gown with an enormous sash that wrapped at the waist and tailed down the back of the gown. The sash itself must have had a million Swarovski crystals. It was featured in Vogue one holiday season with a model holding the gold china cup. Mary would never forget that gown!

"So, wrapping up," Vivian continued while flipping through her yellow note pad, "it's imperative that the *Go Green* collaboration with CJ Nickels is intertwined with the Hot Chocolate Event. There's a lot going on and we cannot afford to disappoint Mr. Heidt. Guys, this is huge. Our customers will have the best HeidtMoore experience on Black Friday that they have ever had!"

Sam raised his hand, as if in a classroom. "Excuse me Vivian, what country will be represented this year for the Hot Chocolate portion?"

"Great question Sam. We have Sloan's great idea, the *Digital Dynasty* that no other department store has access to. This combined with Boggs's *Go Green* initiative introducing CJ Nickels gives customers something of everything. We are expanding that and will promote the event as a global representation. So, no specific country, as the focus will be more worldwide. We want to be inclusive and not exclusive. The hot chocolate will be our own this year."

Pietro piped in. "Yes, the recipe is secret, and worth the experience. Everyone who is anyone will want to be on the guest list. Be sure your associates know what we have to offer. Let's not disappoint Mr. Heidt on his first real personal appearance in over a year."

As the meeting adjourned Mary overheard Vivian whispering to Hilz, "This event better get business back on track. Did you see the online report this morning? Online sales are killing it and they don't even have an IG account yet."

Hilz responded in a loud whisper. "I saw, I still get the emails from corporate. What's it been a year? They still have me on the distro list. Anyway, I know. You're right and it will do. I'm sure. You always do a killer job with our events. We're lucky to have you."

TECH NECK TROUBLES

It was a calm afternoon and Mary was strolling the sales floor. Looking down the main aisle of her floor she saw nothing but heads down, well, except for Trevor. Trevor was one of the top sales associates from the Fine Five floor. He was the ideal Personal Shopper, an expert in fashion, he was friendly, and he was also a little dramatic. From Louisiana, he had moved to Dallas five years prior and quickly became a top seller. His southern accent charmed the ladies of the charity circuit in town. What set him apart in Mary's mind, was how much he used his phone to promote business. Most of the sales associates had become accustomed to browsing the internet instead of browsing for business.

The advances in technology for HeidtMoore was a double-edged sword. It made contacting customers easier, but at the same time it also was an excuse to constantly look at Facebook. The work cell phones were client books, and the expectation was that they were only to be used for that purpose.

The I-Snoop app was supposed to make the selling process easier, allowing for more productivity from the associates. But, as with most advances in the HeidtMoore, I-Snoop usually had some sort of glitch.

Trevor, along with a handful of associates had embraced I-Snoop. His sales quadrupled the first year it launched. He used all the features to his benefit and was able to multi-task on the sales floor. Unfortunately, not everyone had grasped the concept of texting and picture taking, all the while smiling and engaging with people right in front of them. Mary found it super irritating that so many on her team were growing bumps on their necks from having their heads down looking at their phones all the time.

Approaching Trevor, Mary asked what he was working on.

"Hi, any good prospects today?"

"Not yet honey. Oh, but you know, Mrs. Ivory has the gala this weekend. And she forgot about the yoga class. Jesus, take the wheel! So, of course, now I must find a butter yellow yoga pant, shirt, and matching jacket in you know, 30 minutes. Bless her heart."

"Wait we just got in the Terez pant in yellow. It will be perfect, like butta'," Mary replied laughing at her fake accent for the word "butter."

"Show me!"

"It's right here," walking off the aisle into the Athleisure department. On a rack hung yellow yoga pants, along with coordinating sports bras, tank top shirts, lightweight jackets, and running shorts. Mary noticed the hangers were all shoved to one end of the bar and nearly lost it. *What was this place, CJ Nickels?* Taking a deep breath, she grabbed the spandex pant in an XS and handed it to Trevor.

"Honey, it's perfect."

Trevor grabbed the garments and started to walk off, in the direction of his dressing room. "Thanks Mary."

"Don't mention it. Hey, how many people do you have coming to the Hot Chocolate Collaboration Event on Black Friday? I'm trying to get a gauge on how many clients we can expect."

Trevor looked at Mary like she had grown three heads.

"Oh no, honey, my clients would never go for that…*cheap* stuff. Ugh uh. No ma'am." Then changing the conversation back to Mrs. Ivory, "I'll let you know how she likes these. Bye."

Mary couldn't argue. But this posed a problem. If he wasn't inviting any of his clients, would anybody?

Later that afternoon Mary was overseeing the associates in the Digital Dynasty area. Still bothered by Trevor's response to the Hot Chocolate Event she began to question Genius Team.

"Hi Jennifer, how are you today?" Mary asked a sales associate named Jennifer, as she finished showing a client the *Brow Frownisha* gadget. "Does this thing really work?"

"Hi Mary, you bet it works!" Jennifer replied with her big blue eyes wide open. Pointing to the area between her brows. "See no lines."

"After this season I think I will need one of these. How is your clienteling going for the Hot Chocolate Event?"

"Well I have contacted all my customers on the Snoop list. And many of them will be out of town."

"Did you start at the beginning of the list? Because those will be the ones you see the most. We need to get to the customers who haven't been in the store in a while or better yet, new customers who have not experienced a hot chocolate at the HeidtMoore."

"Oh, I did start at the top. I like calling them because they know who I am. I feel weird inviting someone who has no idea who I am."

"That is the point, Jennifer. Remember the philosophy of the HeidtMoore is relationships. Anyone can go to a CJ Nickels and get something from a nobody. But here, we want you to develop a conversation and relationship with your customers, so they know who you are when you do call. And more importantly they like your service and will want to attend anything you invite them to, because they trust you."

Mary couldn't believe the words were just flowing so naturally and smoothly. She had developed so much confidence working at the HeidtMoore. Wishing her mom, Deloris, could have seen her in action. Then, maybe then, Mary would get interested questions about her career when they saw each other on Sundays.

Jennifer seemed motivated and understood the request to start on another list. She excused herself from the aisle and from behind the POS station and began calling another customer. On to the next lucky person, Mary thought as she walked over to Philip. Philip, like Jennifer, was new to the HeidtMoore and just hired for the holiday season. He was a middle-aged man, balding, who always wore a bowtie. Sloan thought he was an ideal candidate for the Genius Team within the Digital Dynasty.

"Philip, how is your clienteling coming along for the Hot Chocolate Event? You know it's a great opportunity for you to sell a ton of the *Hey Babe* smart speakers. Those things are not cheap, and the commission would be amazing."

"Hi Mary, you're so right. I've set a bet with Sloan to sell 50 before Christmas."

"Wow, I hope that happens. What's your plan?"

"I have been sending a text with my digital business card and a short video of how *Hey Babe* works to my new customers. They are all replying. Then I reply back with the invitation to the Black Friday Hot Chocolate Extravaganza."

"That is fantastic, Philip! Thank you for sharing. Remember to only use the HeidtMoore approved evite for the event."

"Oh, I will. Sloan already told me that."

"Well, keep up the great work and I hope you make that goal."

BOGGS BOOTCAMP

The day started as normal. Boggs got up, threw on his tight Nike, fluorescent yellow running shorts, laced up his tennis sneakers, and hit the door running, for his 5:00AM step aerobics, a particularly fast paced, energetic form of working out. This was his custom, every Monday, Tuesday, Thursday, and Friday. After an hour, he would head back to his midcentury modern home and get ready for work. The workouts made Boggs feel energized, especially after he had had two espressos and a protein shake.

Walking into the store, Boggs fist pumped the Loss Prevention team, who politely nodded back. Boggs then walked through Cosmetics, sprayed some Tom Ford cologne, and jumped up the winding escalator, barely glancing at the colorful fish tank. It never failed to amaze him how many magnificent species of sea creatures there were. He watched the majestic multi-colored fish swim about. They swam in unison through the coral reef that ran the height of the circular tank.

By the time he reached the second floor, his phone was ringing. This was pretty typical. In fact, if his phone had not rung by the time he reached the second floor, he would get a nervous twitch. He was expecting Mr. Heidt or one of his sales associates. Probably a customer issue or something. Whatever it was, Boggs was ready to face any challenge, no matter big or small. This was his expertise.

It was Rod.

Lord. Seriously. What now? Boggs did not want to deal with his partner who was thousands of miles away. He was going to start talking about how his life was so wonderful helping poor people. He did not want to deal with it. At all. But the phone kept ringing with Rod's one of a kind ring tone, *'We are the World.'* By Michael Jackson, which Boggs found particularly annoying.

"Hello?" He answered the call, regretfully.

"Hey, hot stuff!", said Rod on the other end, a thousand miles away.

"Don't say that. I'm walking the floor and I have you in speaker."

"Well, take me off, lover."

Boggs took the call off speaker and placed the phone to his ear.

"Yes. What's up?"

"Why are you so upset? I'm only calling to hear your sexy voice."

"Yes, well I'm at work. What is it? If you are calling about wiring more money to you, it's not happening." In the past two months Boggs had wired an estimated three thousand dollars to Rod. He wasn't pleased with sending so much money to him, as the cost of living in Peru was so cheap. When Boggs asked why he needed so much money Rod told him it was for school supplies and Boggs couldn't say no to that. It was a good cause after all.

"I only need a thousand dollars. Please baby. They need it. These people have nothing," Rod pleaded.

"I sent you money already!" Boggs voice starting to rise, catching the attention of a few sales associates standing nearby.

"But honey, that was different."

"How?!"

"That was for the other school."

"How many schools are you giving money to?!"

154

"You make it seem like a bad thing. At least I'm doing something helpful." There it was. The final rub. The thing that made Boggs feel like his retail experience and his day to day was of no consequence. Boggs' eyes scanned the floor, looking for some sort of reassurance that his life at the HeidtMoore did have meaning and purpose.

Meanwhile, the OST staff were busy reticketing merchandise and getting the store ready for opening.

Removing the phone from his ear, Boggs shouted over to the OST staff, or the Optimal Selling Team, as their formal title was called, over in Ladies Shoes.

"Hey! Make sure those Moonboots are on the discounted rack. How many we got?"

"A ton, Chief" answered back Willy, head of the OST team. "It ain't pretty and we're short staffed."

"Again?" The OST team continued to be short staffed and it was causing a lot of problems.

"Yep. We'll be out here on the floor till store close I recon'." That was not a good sign. Mr. Heidt always said that that the magic happened in the store when the mechanics of running the store, like markdowns and ticketing items, was hidden from sight. The public was only allowed to see beauty and not the reality of what it was really like to keep everything looking seamless.

Shit. Boggs hated to hear how items from the previous season hadn't sold. Items he himself had believed in and had wanted to succeed. That was the thing about Boggs. When he believed in something, he really got behind it 100% and such was the case with the Moonboots. The season before this item was the number one item and was promised to be the number one selling item for the company.

Unfortunately, that wasn't the case.

Due to the lack of demand, despite all efforts by Boggs to rally the team, to create selling contests, and even to sell the boots to customers himself, the Moonboots were a dud and failed to sell. Now five hundred pairs of Moonboots sat to one side being marked down. And the OST team, dressed in their dark grey shirts and pants, were going to be out on the floor marking everything with their electronic machines, making beeping noises. It would look more like a prison system than a luxury department store. But Boggs had no choice. There wasn't any time to figure out the logistics of where to put the OST crew and the boots. This was Boggs life! His partner was helping poor children in a third world country and he was dealing with discounted moonboots! It felt to Boggs like his whole life was a series of mismarks.

Distracted for a moment, he forgot that Rod was still on the phone. He had so many things to deal with.

"So, babe, babe? Hello?"

Boggs placed the receiver back to his ear.

"Yes, I'm here. Dealing with the…oh, never mind."

"So, about the money…"

"Yes, Alright. I'll transfer money tonight."

"You're the best!"

Boggs ended the call, put his phone in his pocket and decided his time would be best spent in his office going over the sales reports.

MIXED NUTS

Mr. Pandy Penkins was now a regular customer, coming in weekly to the HeidtMoore. This pleased a lot of people from the sales associates who loved the new commissions they were receiving, to the Executives, mainly Boggs and Sloan, who loved bending over backwards to do anything to keep Mr. Penkins happy.

On Monday and Friday mornings, Mr. & Mrs. Penkins would come into the restaurant at around 10:00am, just when the store opened. They would take breakfast in the Pingüino where they would each have two slices of melon, three eggs each, two cups of coffee and a special Pingüino cheese roll. It wasn't long before they had their own button on the sales register. They never deviated from this order and never asked to see a menu. Even when melons were out of season, the restaurant staff made sure melon was delivered from wherever they might be in season. The Penkins sat at the corner table number 45 overlooking the restaurant. They could look at every customer walking in, which they loved. Promptly at 10:45 a.m., they would leave to go and shop the store. The bill was never presented to them. This was the custom of the top clients of the HeidtMoore.

Mrs. Penkins, who went by "Almond", would meet her associate, Olga, in dresses and shop for a few hours, racking up a bill of several thousand dollars. Olga quickly learned Almond's likes and dislikes. She knew, for instance, Almond loved anything with animal print, but disliked anything with flowers. Olga understood that she wanted to be perceived a certain way and saw it as her duty to help the customer achieve this goal.

Pandy would go to the men's department and meet Zane. They looked over the new suits for the season. He wanted to stand out and he wanted something that no one else had. This was a task Zane was thrilled to take on. He was also able to win him over with the $1000 3oz face cream. Since Mr. Penkins was not a small fellow, he went through the cream faster than the average customer.

In the last month, Mr. & Mrs. Penkins had become what associates referred as a Gold Square level customer. I-Snoop, the electronic device associates used to track sales, and look up customer profiles and ring sales, placed customers into different levels based on spending. With each level, customers received HeidtMoore perks such as free shipping, valet parking, comp meals, salon services and more. Almond Penkins loved the salon nail service and came to the store every week for a mani-pedi. Then she usually spent the afternoon in the Precious Jewelry area coveting the newest diamond collections.

Olga had latched on to Mrs. Penkins shortly after Zane's initial appointment with Pandy. They got along like icing on a cake. Almond loved a good deal and Olga was an expert at finding the special prices or one-of-a-kind pieces. Fortunately for Olga, Almond was an exact size 6. She was the opposite of her husband who wasn't exactly fit. Almond stayed in shape, she said by only eating nuts and cabbage. She insisted that it was her husband's nut products that had changed her life. Almond was his best promoter.

Olga had set aside a few outfits for Almond to try one for the upcoming luncheon at the HeidtMoore. It was a small intimate event for top customers and Olga wanted to make sure Almond Penkins looked her best! Olga knew it would take that long to get the alterations done if anything was needed.

"Almond, I have perfect dress for you. Just in. Only one," Olga said, while practically pulling her customer to the fitting room area.

"Oh, I'm excited to see what you've found. But I would just like to look at Valentino before we start trying on," Almond replied.

"Yes, ma'am. We have new shipment that is not out yet. I will go get for you. Meet you over there," Olga said pointing to the Valentino boutique on the Fine Five floor.

Olga scampered to the backstock room looking for anything in the Valentino section that Almond had not already seen. There was not a new shipment as she had stated. It was a comment Olga made about every designer to any customer that seemed interested.

A few floors down from where Olga was providing the expected personal service, Sarafina was busy overseeing her precious jewelry department, and scanning the RSVP report on Groupies. Sarafina was known for elaborate luncheons in her Precious Jewelry department, so it was the obvious choice for the Turkey Tea this year. She had been working over-time to get everything ready for her Saturday event. Not only would they need tea and hors d'oeuvres, and special jewelry pieces just for the event, but also of course, they needed the HeidtMoore's top customers with the most disposable income.

It was two weeks before Thanksgiving and the number of RSVPs for the afternoon tea was not where it needed to be. The toughest job of all managerial duties at the HeidtMoore was to get customers to actually *attend* the events. Even when customers said they were going to attend and they had taken the time to RSVP, they rarely showed up. And in typical HeidtMoore form lately, there were two important events back to back, making it doubly impossible to book for. The Tea was a much smaller scale, but because it was precious jewelry the event could yield as much of a return or more. The Black Friday Hot Chocolate Event was a huge event, and the same customers were expected to attend both.

"Ally, have you called all your customers? We need people. Let me see your list please," Sarafina said, peering over her shoulder. Ally was the slender, beautiful, forty-something ex model with several marriages behind her. Her haughty attitude made her aloof.

"Of course, I've made the calls. You can't just make them respond," replied Ally, with a bit of an attitude. Knowing it was useless to discuss this any further, Sarafina made her way to the other side of the Precious Jewelry bay, to another one of her associates.

"Liz, you have the Gottrock's transfer coming right? And we need to make sure we have the pieces for the Penkins," Sarafina continued. "I am going to make the rounds and see about gathering more names."

Liz, a woman in her late sixties, had the sort of larger than life personality and oversized physical presence that made most people at the HeidtMoore afraid of her. She also matched her clothing with everyday jewelry she decided to wear.

As usual, she wasn't paying attention to Sarafina. Instead, she was gazing at a massive sparkling diamond ring forced onto one of her fingers. Inspecting her ring, she simply nodded in agreement at whatever it was Sarafina had said.

"Rebecca, who do you have coming for the luncheon?" Sarafina asked the broody red head standing near the office door chomping on a donut.

Wiping her mouth with the back of her hand she answered, "My customers will be there, you know they want that free turkey," she mumbled with a mouth full of food.

"Finish that and get back to the bay. You know if Nacho catches you it will be my ass."

Next, Sarafina headed over to the Handbag department looking for Sparkle. Sparkle, who was at this point five or six months pregnant, was up to her elbows in handbags, barely able to move. It didn't matter that she was expectant with child, she hardly showed. It simply disgusted her manager that she could have let this happen. Tevi couldn't figure out why she would do this to herself. Particularly when there were so many handbags to sell and a department store that needed saving! Sparkle wasn't the best associate, but she wasn't the worst either. To Tevi, this whole pregnancy situation was a great inconvenience.

Tevi had requested that Sparkle remerchandise the Ferramy bags, quite an undertaking. So there Sparkle was, up on a ladder grabbing bags, re-positioning bags, and making sure everything was in order.

"Hi Sparkle, do you need a hand with that?" Sarafina asked, as she saw Sparkle stepping down from a step stool with about 6 handbags flung across her. It was an accident waiting to happen.

"Oh no, thanks, I've got it. Chloe from the buying office is meant to be helping me, but I think I saw her down in Contemporary shopping. Again." Sparkle replied stepping carefully onto the carpet. "Oh well. What's going on?"

"Hopefully, she'll be here soon to help you. I was just following up about the Thanksgiving Tea. It's fast approaching, and we still need more customers. How has your response been?"

"Well I just got a voicemail this morning from Tevi that Mrs. Ivory will definitely be there. She is also bringing a friend."

"That is great news. Keep me posted on your clients please. I will let you get back to this," Sarafina motioned to the pile of handbags on the counter.

Heading up the escalator to find Mary, Sarafina gazed into the fish tank. As she watched the school of fish swimming toward the chunk of food, she wished clients would respond to events this same way. *What if we served some sort of food item? Ah, ha that's it. We need a personalized cookie! I have to remember to tell Vivian!*

Stepping off the escalator, she saw Lulu.

"Lulu, how are you? Do you have a minute?"

"Of course, how are you Sarafina? Are you ready for Thanksgiving? Gobble, gobble!" Lulu said with a cute little chuckle. Lulu had worked in the Gifts & Home department of the HeidtMoore for forty plus years and was well past retirement age. Everyone adored Lulu. She was sweet and had a charming syrupy voice. But not to be fooled. She was also an absolute shark and would do anything to make a sale.

"I'm getting there if I can just get past this event. Then I can focus on a turkey. By the way, do you have anyone attending the Turkey Tea?"

"Yes, my customer from Oklahoma is coming. You know the Smith's come to every HeidtMoore event."

"That's wonderful, Lulu. Thank you. Have you seen Mary?"

"Yes, she was just over in Tech. You know, that's a very strange area of our store", she said menacingly, "I can't imagine why or how that will ever succeed. But what do I know." Sarafina had no time for chatter.

"You never know. I had better be going now. See you later and let me know if you get any other invites to the tea."

Sarafina moved to the Tech area at the opposite end of the sales floor, where she came upon Mary, who was halfway up a ladder fixing the candy cane wall that showcased all the holiday gadgets. *I'm not getting paid enough for this crap. Fixing these damn lights every day is ridiculous. Why do they even bother?*

Interrupting Mary's train of thought, Sarafina approached her, almost making her fall off the ladder.

"Hi Mary!"

"Shit, Sarafina, you scared me to death," laughed Mary.

"What on earth are you doing?"

"Fixing these damn lights for the billionth time!"

"Hey, have you heard from Mrs. Dinkleheimer about the Turkey Tea?"

"Oh, yes, she will be there and is looking forward to it. Did the emerald ring come in? She will want to try it. I know if it fits, it's sold."

"Excellent. I will check and let you know."

After Sarafina had checked with Zane to make sure the HeidtMoore's newest multi billionaire customer, the Penkins, was attending the Turkey Tea, it was time to shop about for herself in the Fine Five department. The Penkins had been spending unimaginable amounts of money recently and while it was somewhat unusual, Sarafina, Sloan and Zane chose to ignore it. Lots of people came into money and would spend heaps of it all at once. This wasn't any different. But who knew you could make so much from the production and distribution of nuts?

A few hours later Olga had finished her appointment and responded to a text from Sarafina. *Almond is set for the tea.* Almond had found a perfect outfit for the Tea, and Olga spent the rest of the day getting the items to alterations and finding the perfect shoe and handbag to match. She would just ring those items knowing Almond would be thrilled.

TURKEY TEA GONE WILD

The Turkey Tea was a new event for the HeidtMoore, created to drive business from the Diamond Club customers. They could sip tea and while looking over the holiday jewelry collections first, and as a gift pick out their own turkey for Thanksgiving. These were not just any turkeys, but the best free-range, organic, heritage turkeys in the United States.

Pietro and his visual team were in the department moving fixtures around preparing for the tea. The afternoon of the Turkey Tea had arrived and Sarafina was feeling nervous. Would the clients show up? More importantly, would they buy? Sarafina was not completely confident that these turkeys would produce the additional sales needed for the season, but she was willing to try anything at this point. What was very unclear was where the live turkeys would be kept during the event. But that was none of her business. She simply had to focus on the jewelry and leave the rest to PR and the visual team.

"We have to create a space for the turkeys," Pietro exclaimed to his crew.

The Precious Jewelry department had been transformed into a Thanksgiving pilgrims' paradise. It had taken Pietro and his team hours to put the event together and move in all of the visuals needed for the day. Rustic chic tables were scattered throughout the area.

"I never want to see another pilgrim belt buckle ever again." Pietro said, as he rushed about adding the finishing touches to the tables. "What do you think? Have I not produced something so beautiful and magical?"

"You've done it again Pietro. I don't know what to say but thank you," said Vivian, sincerely amazed at all of the hard work he had put into the tea. "Oh good! The servers have arrived." She walked off to give them their directions for the day.

The servers, all six of them, wore pilgrim attire, white shirts, black pants, and a large belt with square gold buckles. They were each holding a tray to be filled with various nibbles.

The corner near the ladies' shoe department was immersed with trees and foliage to make the turkeys appear to be in their natural environment. The turkeys had not been released yet but would be once all of the guests had arrived.

Most of the Diamond Club members arrived on time. As they entered the area each guest was promptly offered tea and biscuits. They mingled about looking at the array of precious jewelry.

Zane had come up from the cosmetics department for the afternoon to assist his customers.

"Where are the Penkins?" Sarafina asked Zane.

"They should be arriving any minute."

Within a few minutes Mr. And Mrs. Penkins walked in. Almond wore a Givenchy caftan with the logo motif and monili designs throughout. Mr. Penkins wore a handsome pinstriped custom Brioni suit, paired with a less attractive ebony tie. The design was obviously custom as well because there appeared on the tie, upon close inspection, various hand stitched nuts.

"You look wonderful Mrs. Penkins," Sarafina exaggerated her welcome. "Lovely to see you Mr. Penkins." While they exchanged air kisses. Sarafina glanced over to Vivian and nodded. Vivian received that as a signal and glanced over to Pietro, who took that as a sign to release the turkeys onto the floor, much to the delight of the guests who 'ooohed' and 'ahhhed' over the spectacle.

As the Penkins walked through the showroom, Mary couldn't help but notice the reaction to this eccentric couple from the assembled high net worth customers. Turning their gaze from the turkeys to the Penkins, every person eyed the couple with suspicion, judging the way they looked. The couple seemed unfazed and took a seat by the side of the room, closest to the prized turkeys.

Mary had been in the Van Cleef & Arpels area showing Mrs. Dinkleheimer, a formidable oil heiress and landowner, the coveted Zip necklace. It was 18kt yellow gold dripping with diamonds and cabochon tear drop shaped emeralds.

"Mary, what do you think?" Mrs. Dinkleheimer asked, posing with the necklace on. Before Mary could respond, she continued, "Wait, is that Pandy over there?" She motioned to the turkey corner. Mary looked over.

"Yes, Mr. & Mrs. Penkins, do you know them?"

"Yes, we go way back. He is the king of nuts you know. They sell more fruitcakes and nuts in a month than you all sell lipsticks in a year!"

Mary figured the statement was probably close to the truth because Sarafina was at the last manager meeting speaking about their spend levels.

In another area of the room, Mrs. Ivory and her guest had just arrived. She shrugged off her pink mink wrap, just in time for Tevi to catch it. Mary recognized her guest as the same man who attended the play with Mrs. Ivory.

"Tevi darling, would you be so kind as to make sure Roberto and I are not seated with that couple," requested Mrs. Ivory, as she subtly nodded towards the Penkins.

"Do you mean the Penkins'?"

"Yes, sweetheart, I don't want to bore Roberto with the conversations about nuts and fruit, if you know what I mean. We want to keep his focus on the important things at hand."

"I completely understand Mrs. Ivory, not a problem at all."

Tevi quickly walked over to Sarafina. "Make sure those bloody Penkins people are not at the same table as Ivory and her secret, not so secret lover! I need sales today and do not want it fucked up by those nutty people."

Sarafina went to find Vivian to make sure the seating arrangements were fixed accordingly. As the guests were seated Sloan welcomed the elite crowd with a short speech about the history of the HeidtMoore and how Mr. Heidt wanted to be there for the event but was not feeling well. He ended the introduction by walking over to the live turkeys saying, "Time to eat!" At the same time, the turkeys, as if on cue started clucking. Pietro gently herded them back to their pen.

Several hours later the meal was finished, and the customers had enjoyed viewing the extravagant jewelry. It was customary for clients of this caliber not to purchase the day of the event. They usually ogled over the items and then would send an assistant in at a later time to pick up the selected items.

Unfortunately, halfway through the presentation, two of the turkeys escaped the pen and started flapping their wings and started running about the floor. They caused such a commotion that several of the customers took this as their cue to leave the event.

"Don't go yet. Let me show you one more piece. Also, don't forget you get a free turkey too!" Sarafina practically pleaded with several of her clients not to go anywhere but at least stay until she had displayed all of the jewelry.

"Another time. This was nice but we need to leave."

The turkeys were making so much noise it was very distracting. Not to mention the mess they were making on the sales floor.

Pietro tried to catch one of the turkeys that had escaped the coop. He was all arms and legs trying to catch the rogue bird, distressing Mrs. Ivory who quickly left without any of the birds she was entitled to take.

"We can deliver to your house if you would like?" Mary said helpfully.

"No, no, that's quite alright," she said, picking up her stole, and her date and leaving the store.

The event ended and Sarafina felt like crying. What a disaster! Pietro was covered in turkey feathers and the floor was covered in turkey poop. Vivian was instructing the waiters and housekeeping to clean up. The event had not been a success at all!

PARTY ON PARTY PEOPLE

Events for customers at the HeidtMoore were always on the calendar, but celebrations for associates were few and far between. There seemed to be little in the way of appreciation events. In fact, since Mary started working at the department store, she had only witnessed one fun function for employees, and that was the annual HeidtMoore Talent Show. She had assumed it was due to the sheer size of the store that employees weren't recognized more often.

Little did Mary know that the employees took it upon themselves to create celebrations. The store needed some sort of 'fun committee". Perhaps she could bring this idea up to Brandi on their next "touch base" meeting. Whenever that might be! Brandi had been missing in action for a while now. But fun committee or not, there were big "employee-only" events in December; the Alterations Luncheon and a more private, 'by invitation only' party hosted by Ta'Keisha. This was the big Christmas celebration she held each year for her friends on the Cosmetics floor.

The day of the Alterations party, Boggs met Sloan in his office. They would attend the party together to show unity. Upon arriving in the alterations room, they were greeted by about twenty workers. None of them were from the United States. The room was cramped and filled with garments and rolling racks. Hanging from the ceiling were multiple colored streamers and other Christmas, decorations including in the corner, a plastic Father Christmas.

Good Lord. Sloan muttered under his breath. This was his least favorite holiday party. He didn't like the cheap decorations and he was not a fan of the fake Santa. The hardest part was swallowing the food. One year the alterations team served fried crickets in hotdog rolls. He bit into one by accident mistaking the crickets for bits of beef. As soon as he heard the crunch, he quickly excused himself and ran to the bathroom.

Boggs was happy to dig into whatever the workers gave him. Sloan, on the other hand, practically gagged when he arrived in the room. Until he saw a box he thought looked familiar.

"These dumplings are so good. Where are they from?"

"They from My PhoKing Dumplings, on Northwest Highway." *Great! Something reliable*, thought Sloan as he made a bee line for the box of dumplings.

This was the alterations holiday party. Every dish imaginable from Southeast Asia was on the table; two different types of yellow colored dumplings, four giant plates of fried rice, multiple unrecognizable fried meat dishes, and Jell-O mousse plates in various fluorescent colors.

"You will like very much. You try this," said Van, the head seamstress. Originally from Vietnam, she had been at the HeidtMoore for twenty years. She was fierce and domineering and associates and managers alike were very afraid of her. So, when she placed a plate of meat in front of Sloan, he was reluctant to say no, although he desperately wanted to. He had never seen meat cooked that way before.

"Van, how was this prepared? It looks so…appetizing." Asked Sloan, trying his best to remain grateful. Born in the south, his mother had always taught him the importance of manners.

"You like? You like?" A smile upon her face, Van forced the plate into Sloan's hands. Taking the dish, he smiled and went to the long table set up in the room and took a seat on one of the folding chairs.

Half of the HeidtMoore managers were already sitting at the table, eating, and talking to the alterations team. There was Moon, from China, a sweet, sophisticated alterations lead. He worked in men's suiting and dressed impeccably. The same could not be said for the other people who worked in alterations. There was Man, a Vietnamese woman, in her late forties, who wore tight, ill-fitting dresses in various patterns of floral. She took care of the bridal alterations. She was renowned for her nimbleness as well as her cooking, but not her dress sense. She cooked for the team every Friday.

Sloan mustered up the courage to take a bite of his meal. Van was watching him with her beady eyes. He staked the meat with his folk. It was tough. He slowly moved the folk up to his mouth, took a deep breath and put it in his mouth. It was hard to chew.

"Ah. You eat dog. So brave!" said Moon. Sloan immediately started coughing and spit out the rest. This was the worst day of his life.

Ta'Keisha meanwhile was throwing her own party in the Moore room, a private room on the fourth floor typically used for top client luncheons or executive meetings. Not today. Today was Ta'Keisha's day. She had saved up all her money the whole year to throw her "Christmas Hip Hop Ho Down" party for her friends and fellow associates. She rented the hot pink linens, purchased the food, which consisted of fried chicken and grits, the hip hop party decorations and printed the invitations to her guests.

"Sista' girl! Hang that streamer up there," she said to Zane, pointing up at the ceiling. A few of the beauty associates had come up to the room to help Ta'Keisha set things up. The décor was Christmas ghetto fabulous. Within an hour the room was set and ready to go. Multi-colored tissue streamers draped from each of the elaborate chandeliers. Fake carnations replaced the real orchids that were in the room. For extra effect, Zane tossed fake dollar bills around the room, then shouted, much to Ta'Keishas delight, "Let's make it rain."

The room soon filled up with associates from throughout the store, although mostly from the beauty department. Now that ABBI and her beauty bots had taken over, leaving the floor wasn't nearly as difficult.

From the Bose system set up in the back of the room, 90's hip hop and R&B played. As soon as Notorious B.I.G started playing, everyone got up from their seats and started dancing. Within an hour the dancing became a little more raucous. By the time Montel Jordan "This is how

171

we do it" played, the dancing turned into grinding. At which point, Sloan conveniently appeared and closed the party down.

Good Lord this is outrageous, thought Sloan. When he saw Zane dancing away with his coiffed hair and five shades of foundation on his glistening face, Sloan took another look. Zane was dressed in his tight white Tom Ford shirt and Sloan couldn't hide the fact that he wished he were dancing too. Long gone were the days when Sloan would go clubbing. The music, although not his style, was making him long for a time that was easier. Literally. A time when he could get any guy he wanted. Now, no one even glanced his way. Not even on Flasher, a new gay dating app he had just joined.

He snapped out of his daydream.

"Ok, that's enough. Back to the floor. Get selling. We have big goals, and we need to sell two million every day. Well, we won't be doing that by...twerking." He spat out the last word with great distain in his voice.

"Ok boss, we are cleaning up now," Ta'Keisha yelled out from the back corner of the room. "Come 'on y'all help me with this cake. Take a piece with you." She walked over to Sloan. "Boss you know you want a slice," laughing.

"Can't. No gluten until New Year."

SLOAN SURVEYS THE STORE

A few days later in the late afternoon Sloan was walking the store. He was pleased with the way everything looked. Feeling in a festive mood, he started wearing his favorite Christmas tie, a custom-made Dior tie in red and green stripes. This tie, he believed, brought him good luck as it had been handed to him by Mr. Heidt Senior. A fact he shared often. Walking through the departments, he walked with a pep in his step. *Today was going to be a good day.*

The store was looking exceptionally good. Each holiday decoration glittered, and every fixture dazzled. This was going to be the best Christmas ever. Particularly if Sloan became the new General Manager. That was his dream. To be able to run the HeidtMoore department store. It was all within his reach.

First, as General Manager, Sloan would insist all employees work an extra hour more a day. He would also make sure that every associate was given a specific task to complete, like sell five items a day from a different area of the store. So, if an associate were in Mens, they would have to sell five things from epicure. He figured he may get push back at first, but it was the only way to get the store to produce the numbers needed to be super successful. Also, it was about time the employees stopped being so lazy. At least this was his opinion. It didn't matter that the majority were struggling to make ends meet. He thought this was their fault and not the fault of competitors and online shopping. Oh no, with Sloan at the helm, this store was going to be in tip-top shape in no time at all. Unfortunately, it was this mentality that did not endear him to his staff.

Sloan needed to plot *how* he was going to take full control of the HeidtMoore.

While it was true Mr. Heidt was still in charge and thankfully still alive, Sloan could not see how much longer he could really manage as General Manager of the world's most famous department store. There had been too many scandals, too many missed days of work, and too many lies. Mr. Heidt had been so evasive for so long, not attending meetings, not even showing up to the store. While he may have been found in a rehab facility, he was in no rush to return to the HeidtMoore. Even when he said he would be available on a call, he rarely was. The whole situation was strange. What the store needed was a manager who could be trusted and admired. Sloan was that man. He arrived to work early and stayed late. Unlike Boggs he did not have any other obligations or distractions. Sloan's life *was* the HeidtMoore.

In the Gifts & Home area, one of his favorite departments, Sloan saw a need to call housekeeping. He noticed there was dust on some of the shelves carrying fine china. *Outrageous*, he thought. Then he texted Antonio. "Come to Fine China, now. Dust on the shelves."

Antonio, the head of housekeeping, was in a storage room that acted as his office on the first floor. Antonio was a handsome Latino man in his early thirties, who managed a small team of twenty – far too small a team to be able to clean the entire store. Generally, Antonio loved his job and tried to do his best. But he didn't much like the executives in the store, who treated him as little more than a peasant. While he didn't let it bother him too much, it was annoying, and he had heard more than a few grumblings from his team. One housekeeper did walk out the season prior. If Antonio could provide for his family of six and put food on the table, then he was a happy man.

He was eating soup and watching Spanish tv on his phone when Sloan's message came through. Disgusted by the message he had received he pushed his soup aside.

"El es stupido." he muttered, rolling his eyes. As he hit reply, he typed in the devil emoji. As tempted as he was to hit send, he quickly erased the image and simply typed: BE RIGHT THERE.

Getting up from his orange plastic chair, he picked up a can of cleaning solvent and a rag, then left to attend to the dusting issue in Fine China. By the time he reached his destination, Sloan was nowhere to be seen. Neither was the dust he texted about. Another waste of time for poor Antonio.

Sloan had ventured down to the Cosmetics department to see how his beauty bots were doing.

Not very well by the looks of things.

One bot had malfunctioned and had been moved to the side, off the sales floor. Another one, behind the Bobbi Brown counter was frozen. And still another near the LaMer counter was not working. The bot's left arm manically kept applying bronzer into a blank space, while its head tilted to one side saying, "look-in good. Beaut-i-ful. Look-in good. Beaut-i-ful." Over and over.

"Make it stop. My God!" Screeched Zane, as he pulled Sloan to the side to take a look at it.

"What on earth happened?" asked Sloan, shooting Zane an accusatory look, as though he purposely broke the beauty bot.

"Don't look at me! All I was doing was trying to service a client. Ugh. I knew these bots were never going to work. This place is going downhill. How am I meant to sell under these conditions? It's going to be Christmas, and nothing works!"

"You sold perfectly fine before the bot. You can sell fine now. What's the big deal? Go back to the sales floor. I'll sort this out," he said, looking to see where there might be a battery pack Sloan could take out. Unfortunately, there were no directions on how to solve a beauty bot mechanical issue.

"Why do we even have them in the first place?"

That was a question Sloan honestly couldn't answer. He had played a major role in the beauty bot buying process. But now he was beginning to question the reasons for his decision.

Sloan stopped and looked at Zane.

"They are a great asset to our company and to you, if you don't break them."

"That's so unfair! This company used to be about the people, and now it's about bots! I've had it!" And he stormed off, back to the department.

Sloan wondered briefly if Zane's remark meant he was quitting the HeidtMoore. He followed after Zane to see if he would take the escalator up to HR or not. This would not be good for Sloan if Zane quit. The more employees under Sloan's leadership at the store, who quit because of him, the less of a chance he would have for being General Manager. It wouldn't look good. And Zane being a top book, it really wouldn't look good. The company needed Zane. Sloan needed Zane.

He watched carefully to see what he would do.

Sloan was saved. For now. Pandy Penkins had just arrived and Zane was making a beeline, across the floor, to the customer. He texted Antonio again. *After dusting, come to Cosmetics. Three Bots down.* Then he went up to the Ladies Shoes area. Typically, this department was for Boggs to oversee but Sloan liked to browse through all the departments subtly comparing with his counterpart. The department looked immaculate. Each shoe was perfectly placed on library shelves. The entire area looked ready for a photo shoot. The only thing missing were customers.

HOT CHOCOHOLIC EVENT IN HOT WATER

Everyone was so excited for *the* event of the season! After so much hard work and so little time to get the word out about the collaboration, Boggs was feeling pretty confident this set him up nicely to become the next HeidtMoore General Manager.

Sloan was also feeling confident that his ingenious idea for innovative technology gadgets would put his name on the map to become the next General Manager. It was becoming increasingly apparent that Mr. Heidt had little interest in staying much longer in his position. Today would be Mr. Heidt's first day back in the store, in over a year. At some point during the day's festivities, Sloan planned on having a private meeting with his boss to discuss his future.

It was 9:00am in the store and Mr. Heidt had not arrived yet. This wasn't unusual as he was known for strolling in at around eleven or twelve, even on important event days.

Vivian was running around frantically.

"Hey, you have the hot chocolate ready, right?" She said walking through to the kitchens of the HeidtMoore. Since Chefs departure, Vivian had been worried as to how they would execute the food and drink for the events. Brandi had not hired anyone to fill the executive chef role for the store.

One of the kitchen staff showed Vivian the large vat of hot chocolate. She was satisfied with what she saw. She had a taste and made her way to the front of the Pingüino restaurant. The tables had been set the night before according to her specifications. Approving everything, she headed down the escalator. On to the next task of the day, the physical set up of the event.

On the main floor of the Cosmetics department, where the giant gold entranceway to the store was located, Vivian and Pietro had worked together to create an opulent walkway, through the department. One gold runner ran the length of the department and on either side were glass tiers with the *Go Green* and *Digital Dynasty* products. Flanking the winding escalator and the giant fish tank, were the CJ Nickels clothing items and various other products.

When the customer proceeded up the winding escalator to the second floor, they would be able to view all the merchandise, while in the background exotic fish swam around. The second-floor entrance was also covered with a gold runway leading to the Hot Chocolate fountain set up between Precious Jewelry and Handbags. While the department was vast, it was still a challenge for Pietro to determine how to make the space not feel cramped. There was so much merchandise being brought down from the fourth floor. He attached, with invisible wire, the CJ Nickels merchandise from the ceiling. No expense was spared, and the overall effect was like one from a couture exhibition at a museum.

Mary was busy preparing for the event, checking off her to-do list and sipping her Starbucks latte.

"I was inspired by the Dior exhibit and Alexander McQueen show at the Met. This will be a day no one will forget. Mary, what do you think?" said Pietro, approaching Mary.

They both turned to look up at the elaborate designs Pietro had just installed, hanging from the ceiling.

"It's magnificent!" Mary instinctively knew that Pietro needed his ego stroked. She stood in awe at the incredible work he had done, gazing at the beautiful visual displays before her. Each piece looked so much more expensive than it really was. In fact, individually, each piece of clothing looked pretty awful. *Who was going to buy a black trash liner dress?* But it was all in the presentation and Pietro understood this all too well.

Once the eyes took in the apparel, the next shock was the elaborate chocolate fountain surrounded by food delights and fine china cups. Customers for the event would gather in this department for the big toast.

By eleven o'clock, everything was set up for the hot chocolate event and the team was ready. CJ Nickels had arrived, the managers were all in attendance, and Boggs and Sloan were making sure each piece in their respective initiatives looked perfect.

"Have you heard from Mr. Heidt?" Sloan asked Vivian. He wasn't going to ask Boggs. That would be a sign of weakness.

"Not a thing. He better be here. I'm over it! Ask Boggs."

Sloan asked a few more people before finally having to ask Boggs. Approaching his nemesis, biting his lip, Sloan walked up to Boggs, who was arranging the *Marry Me Juana* weed canisters on a shelving display. Sloan inhaled, then asked Boggs the question, reluctantly.

"He sent a message saying he'd be here in an hour."

"But he's doing the opening speech?" Sloan felt panicked.

"Dunno what to tell ya. I'll do it I guess."

Over my dead body. Thought Sloan.

"I have something I can say." Quickly trying to come up with something.

"CJ Nickels and I already have something lined up. You can close the event."

Ugh. Of course, he's got CJ Nickels. Sloan didn't think much of the retailer, so he was happy if Boggs wanted to stand up and make a fool of himself next to the lower priced Nickels. *Ridiculous.*

Now all they needed were the customers.

At eleven thirty, the associates had lined up along either side of the gold carpet, throughout both the cosmetics main entrance and again on level two just off the escalator, waiting for the herds of people to arrive.

They didn't.

By eleven forty-five, a few customers trickled in. One of them, was Pandy Penkins. Dressed from head to toe in a designer suit with nut motifs, Penkins stood out from the rest of the crowd. If people didn't know he was the king of nuts, they would now. His lapel was open, exposing expensive looking thick, gold chains around his neck. On each one of his perfectly manicured fingers were gold and ruby rings of varying sizes but all equally rich looking. He carried a walking cane; the top of the cane was an enamel walnut. He was certainly a sight to behold. No one could take his eyes off him. Zane was ready to attack any associate who might get close to him. *Hell no, Pandy was his and no one else's.* Associates knew 'money' when it walked through the door.

On instruction for the event, Boggs had told the associates to clap whenever anyone entered the store. When the few trickled in, they clapped vigorously, as if it might draw crowds. It didn't. Boggs had even made everyone practice clapping right before opening. He loved getting his associates motivated before big events. This was his gift.

Mr. Nickels greeted every customer. Meeting Pandy Penkins for the first time, they discovered a mutual love of NASCAR and Pandy managed to get a deal to sell his nuts at all one hundred and forty Nickels stores around the US. He did not, however, purchase any of the collaboration merchandise.

"If he's not buying any of this, who will?" said Sarafina, picking up a black recycled dress from a hanging rod.

So far, the event was a bust.

At twelve thirty, Mr. Heidt had still not shown up and Mary was starving. She called T who was in the executive offices manning the telephones.

"Want to take a break and grab a snack? Nothing is going on down here. It's dead."

"That's bad, who is down there?"

180

"A few people I've never seen, plus managers and associates. Oh, and Pandy is here." Mary scanned the room. "Linda Langley is here, she just arrived. So basically, we've got more staff and press than we do customers. Is it too early to drink?"

"Meet you near the freight. I have one more report to finish for Boggs, then I'll be down."

They took a small break and went back to the floor. It was 1:30 p.m. and the crowd had not grown. In fact, if anything, Mary thought there were fewer people.

"Where have you been?", asked Sloan in a whiny voice.

"I had to step away. I figured it was better to go now versus when everyone gets to the event."

"Fat chance that will happen. This is awful. Where is everyone?"

"No idea. At least we'll have lots left to drink." Mary was looking forward to trying the hot chocolate.

A couple hours went by, unnervingly quietly for an event day.

It was mid-afternoon and Vivian came rushing through with two flutes of champagne. Mary looked to see who she was going to. It was a group of ladies who appeared to be out of place. They were wearing ripped jeans with large diamante belt buckles and plaid shirts. Most were sporting the original *Karen* haircut. Mary deducted they must be CJ Nickels clientele. Vivian came racing back down the aisle.

"New customers. We have to keep them occupied. Every single body counts."

Mary replied, "Oh, how can I help?"

"Get an associate over to them quick. Anyone. Well not anyone. Where is Trevor?"

"I'll text him now."

"Thanks!" Vivian yelled as she headed up the escalator.

Thirty minutes later, Vivian and several managers corralled what few customers were there around the hot chocolate fountain. Mr. Heidt was nowhere to be seen. In order not to disappoint the two influencers who were present and Linda Langley, the show had to go on as they say.

Boggs and CJ Nickels stood in front of the fountain, each with a cup of hot chocolate. "Happy Holidays everyone. And thank you for joining us for this annual event. I would like to introduce a special guest to the HeidtMoore…" Then as if on cue there was a commotion in the aisle of the department. That was when the police showed up, followed by Nacho who was leading them into the department.

"Good grief!" Sarafina was very annoyed. They certainly had not come to buy any PJ. Boggs and Sloan instantly came over to the policemen. The managers and the few customers who were around the hot chocolate fountain turned to stare at the men, like they were intruding on their own private party. *What did they want?*

Mary walked over to Nacho. She loved him doing his job. His handcuffs hanging from his pants, his old-fashioned walkie talkie, his tight shirt, and serious expression. This was not the time for Mary to feel flustered.

"What's happening?", she asked pulling Nacho to one side, while Sloan and Boggs talked to the officers.

"Mary, not now." Before brushing her away with his hand, he gave her a wink. *This must be serious* Mary thought.

Before anyone knew what was happening, Pandy Penkins was in hand cuffs and being taken out of the store.

"Now there's been a mistake! Don't ya' know who I am?"

"We know exactly who you are."

"I'm the king a' nuts. You can't arrest me!" But the policemen didn't pay any attention to him. Watching everything unfold, it was shocking to see. Here was one of the HeidtMoore's best customers being taken away by the police. *Surely this was some mistake?* Zane jumped in and tried to pull Pandy away, but Sloan and Boggs pulled him back. They couldn't afford to have Zane arrested.

"But you can't take Pandy away. We haven't finished ringing his digital dynasty products!" Zane cried, as Pandy was being escorted out of the department. Boggs and Sloan were restraining Zane from going after them.

Boggs grabbed Zane by the shoulders.

"Take it easy." Trying to calm him down. "We'll get to the bottom of this. We will, but you have to wait and see what happens."

"Wait and see? Are you out of your mind? I'd just convinced him to purchase some of the shitty tech items and had put about 15 grand to the side. Now what? I'm so poor." Zane could be overly dramatic. "And stop holding on to my shoulder, this is a YSL jacket for God's sake!" With that he sulked away.

"I always knew there was something funny going on with that man." Leigha, the ladies shoe manager said aloud, who happened to be standing next to Hilz, who was also very opinionated.

"Oh, I knew from the moment I saw him that he was no good. Any man who makes that kind of money from nuts IS nuts."

"I wonder what happened?" Mary was dying to find out.

"Text your boyfriend!"

"Ssh. He isn't my, he's just a, he, we are just you know…" Mary was at a loss for words. She didn't know what Nacho was to her anymore. It had been a while since their relationship talk.

"What? Friends? Okay. Whatever!" Leigha laughed. She loved giving Mary a hard time.

"Whatever he is, we need to know." Hilz said, getting to the point. "This is too good."

Sarafina, standing to the side by the escalator, keeping her distance from everyone, was not amused. "Well, there goes our last resource for selling anything today."

THE BLACKEST FRIDAY

The event at the HeidtMoore made the front page headlines the next morning.

ARREST AT THE HEIDTMOORE. PANDY PENKINS, KING OF NUTS, IS TAKEN INTO CUSTODY FOR FRAUD.

It was shocking. No one could believe the arrest, least of all, Zane.

Sitting at the granite countertop of his uptown condo, drinking a morning veggie shake and wearing a Versace white terry cloth robe, he opened the morning newspaper. Linda Langley was not painting a pretty picture. Zane was panicking as he read the article. The Perkins had embezzled nearly 20 million from their own company! Linda even mentioned the amount they had spent at the HeidtMoore. What would happen to his commission on 5 million dollars? *For fucks sake!* He thought to himself. Would he have to pay back the money from everything he had sold to his customer? This would be a disaster. Not only that, what if Zane had to go to court to testify? Zane had heard of an associate who had to do that once. They had become embroiled in a huge lawsuit with a client who was a leader of an infamous Mexican drug cartel. After he was arrested by the feds the associate was forced to pay back the commission on two years of purchases.

Back at the store, it was not a pretty sight. The sales from the Hot Chocolate Event had been terrible. In fact, the event had been the worst performing event in the HeidtMoore's history. Not only that, the HeidtMoore's brand new, multi billionaire customer had just been arrested. Now what? This was the chance to get back on track again. Not fly off the railway lines!

How did it happen? Why did it all go so wrong? Where were the customers? Boggs, who was normally so upbeat and positive, was downcast and moody. He walked through the cosmetics department, looking at all of the merchandise on the floor that needed to be put back to their rightful place on the fourth floor. Hardly anything had sold. It was 8:00am and Boggs felt sick to his stomach. He didn't know how he would get through the day.

At least Mr. Heidt hadn't shown up to view the debacle. Or was that a bad sign. *Did he know the event would be a disaster?* Boggs couldn't be sure. All he knew was the sinking feeling in his stomach would not go away. He tried to call Rod, who was still in Peru. He just needed someone to talk to, a shoulder to cry on. Rod was always there for him. But there was no answer, as usual. Boggs hadn't been able to get ahold of him in days, in fact. The only reason he knew Rod was okay was because he was still posting pictures on his popular Instagram account, with its 2,000 followers.

Feeling even more disappointed, Boggs put his phone down on one of the glass top counters and then started doing jumping jacks on the sales floor.

Mary and T walked in from the employee entrance, then stopped to stare at Boggs, who was frantically jumping up and down, arms waving back and forth.

"Is he alright?" T asked Mary.

"I'm scared. Something tells me this is a bad sign when he's this ramped up." Mary was not entirely sure how to handle Boggs. All she knew was that Boggs doing vigorous exercises first thing in the morning did not bode well.

Boggs stopped and composed himself as soon as he saw T and Mary coming towards him.

"What's up girls?", he said in a higher than necessary voice.

"Morning. I guess we'll start by putting the china cups that didn't sell back on floor four?" said Mary, acting as if everything was normal. Boggs frowned and put his head down.

"Sure. Whatever." Boggs was forlorn, almost zombie like. Mary wished she were like this anytime she did a bit of exercise.

"Do you need an Advil?" T offered.

"Yes, thank you T. That might help. I hope."

Mary glanced at T.

"I'll be right back."

"Boggs. I'm sorry. I really tried to get every associate on board. We all called so many people, we did."

"I just don't get it. Nothing sold. Not even the Juana gadget. And then the police and the arrest, I just, I don't know. I'm honestly not sure we can survive this."

"Not sure we can survive this?"

"It's looking like the end, Mer. I know. You came here with high hopes. It's every girl's dream to work at the HeidtMoore department store. It was my dream too. And now look. Nothing is what it appears to be after all. We aren't the glamorous put together store we appear to be. It's all so sad."

Mary couldn't believe what she was hearing.

"Come on Boggs. It was one event. We'll get back on track. So what if we lost some sales? And had no customers." The more Mary was trying to make her boss feel better, the more she was starting to realize it probably *was* the end of the department store. She continued. "And our top client got arrested." She was not doing a good job at making Boggs feel better. Taking him by both arms she gently shook him. "Look! We're are going to be fine. We will! You hear me?"

"You are always the optimist, Mer. Thank you." That was the pot calling the kettle black.

Mary really felt sorry for him. She knew he had put his heart and soul into this event. On the plus side, things could only get better, surely.

They both got to work, tidying up what was left of the event. Housekeeping, led by Antonio, came to the floor, and the visual team dismounted the hanging fixtures and chocolate fountain. More managers had started to arrive for the day and began grabbing the merchandise that belonged in their areas. Soon it looked as if Black Friday had never happened.

Sparkle, who was now all belly, was moving slowly across the floor. She finally approached Mary, who was standing at the Bio Beauty counter checking email on her phone.

"I have come to help put the merchandise back."

"That's sweet Sparkle. Talk to Boggs. Not sure where he wants it. Most of what is left is back by the freight elevator. How are you feeling today?"

"Pretty good!" Mary thought this was probably a lie. Sparkle looked like she hadn't slept in days and her face was unusually red and blotchy. As much as Mary wanted to ask how Sparkle was really doing and if she and Chef were still together, now was probably not a good time.

"Okay. Well, take it easy ok? If you need anything, just let me know."

"I will thanks. You're always so great. Tevi doesn't." Cutting herself off from speaking further.

"Tevi doesn't, what?"

"It doesn't matter." Then the tears streamed down her face. "She doesn't care! She thinks I'm the reason for the bad sales."

The tears turned to sobs and Boggs rushed over immediately to see what all the crying was about. This was all he needed.

"Don't cry Sparkle. Everything is going to be fine. You got this kid." Then slapping her on the shoulder he made her tumble forward, just catching herself on a cosmetics chair which helped steady her balance.

"Boggs be careful!" Mary couldn't believe he did that.

"I'm fine. Don't worry. I just need to go over there to sit down."

"Good idea. Go sit down." Boggs said, visually pissed that his associate was leaving to sit down when there was so much work to be down.

As Sparkle waddled off, in her Alice and Olivia paisley moo moo, Boggs took Mary aside.

"Did you see the online business?" He asked her.

"No. But surely they didn't do that well. They didn't have half the inventory we had. At least that's what was in the business report."

"Wrong."

"What?"

"Mer. Truth is, I don't think we're going to make it. Online is beating us in sales by like, one hundred and ten percent. It ain't pretty. We won't rebound."

"But you don't know that."

"Just got a text from Mr. Heidt."

"You did? Why wasn't he at the event?" It made Mary very cross that the general manager not only didn't show up to the biggest event of the year but also apparently offered nothing by way of support for his employees. Mary flashed back to the thought of Heidt Sr. and her mother and how poorly he had treated her. This obviously was a strain that ran through the family.

"That's the least of your worries now. Check this out. Heidt has told me what he plans to do." Boggs showed her his phone.

THERE'S NO WAY OUT!

This did not sound good. At all.

"What is Mr. Heidt saying? What does this mean?"

Just as Mary was about to scroll up, to read the rest of the text message, screams were heard. It sounded like an animal in pain. *My God! What is that?* Boggs and Mary looked at one another in a state of panic.

"Help! Help!" It was Sparkle. Her screams could be heard throughout the store.

"My water's broken!"

Boggs and Mary rushed upstairs to the second floor where they found Sparkle, laying on the floor next to the YSL handbag case line. Boggs immediately called the ambulance. Mary called Nacho. Within minutes Nacho was assisting Sparkle. T arrived with warm tea and a heated towel. Curious had arrived on the scene too, squealing and hopping about.

Boggs tried coaching Sparkle through various breathing techniques he had used to teach his cheerleaders back in the day. His adrenaline kicking in.

"After me deep breath in…. deep breath out. Deep breath in…. Come on, you got this. Okay? Can you hear me?"

"She's in labor Boggs, not going into cardiac arrest," said T. Boggs paid no attention. T texted Tevi to let her know what had happened.

"Bloody nightmare. Glad I'm not there. This is the last thing we need." Was the response Mary got back.

By the time the ambulance had arrived to carry Sparkle away, it was time for the store to open for business.

"Should one of us go with her?" Asked Mary. Boggs had other plans.

"No, you need to stay here and greet our customers and make sure the store is immaculate. I'll send Nacho with her."

Everything from the event had been taken down and all of the merchandise was in its proper place by noon that day. The only thing missing were customers. It was as if Black Friday drained what was left of the customers. It was the complete opposite of how traditional Black Fridays usually were. They would begin the spending sprees and help over-achieve store goals.

Boggs received updates throughout the afternoon from Nacho who was at the hospital.

"Sparkle is in stable condition. False alarm."

"Thanx for update. Make sure she's hydrated and see you when you get here."

"Good advice! OMG, I'll be sure to tell the doctors. I'm sure they didn't think of that." Nacho said sarcastically.

While Nacho was waiting on Sparkle to be released, he wandered through the Labor & Delivery unit of the hospital. Passing by the window of the newborn babies he paused. He saw rows and rows of little babies swaddled. In the far corner there was a father holding his new daughter in his arms. The mom was in a chair just beside the bassinet smiling lovingly up at them. *It is time for me to settle down. This is what it's all about.* His tender moment was interrupted by the doctor. Clipboard in hand, the doctor taking care of Sparkle approached Nacho.

"Hi there! So, I have some good and bad news."

"Oh hi, what?" Nacho said, momentarily forgetting he was here as moral support for Sparkle. The doctor eyeing the newborns replied, "Cute, aren't they? Sparkle's will be here soon. The good news is that she is doing great. The bad news is that the baby won't come for another week."

"What? She has to come back next week?"

"Ha ha. One more week isn't long. Your life is about to change!" The doctor exclaimed.

"Me? Ah ha! Oh no. Definitely not the father," Nacho replied. "Just here to make sure Sparkle is alright. Will she be released today?"

"Yes, just a few more minutes. She will need to stay on bed rest though for the rest of her pregnancy." The doctor headed back into the patient area. Nacho texted Boggs the update. Then he sent Mary a quick text, *Check your Facebook. I changed my status to Fully Devoted.* 😊 *In a relationship. Dinner at 7, my place.*

The days following the Hot Chocolate Event at the HeidtMoore seemed quiet compared to previous years after Black Friday. With only one associate working in her department and several other associates quitting or finding other means of employment in the recent months, Tevi was having to do more work than ever. Human Resources was also having a hiring freeze so Sparkle would not be replaced and there would be no chance of getting any help.

"For fuck's sake. That bloody girl." Tevi said to Mary, stopping by her office upon arrival to the store.

"Come on Tevi. She's having a baby! This is wonderful."

"Wonderful my ass. It's a joke! How am I supposed to sell all this crap?!"

"Tevi. You're jaded, my friend. I thought you would have been here earlier?"

"Nope. Mid-shift. I've never been more grateful to arrive in the store for a bloody mid-shift."

"I've got to get back upstairs to my floor. You are not the only one with associate issues," chuckling, Mary left the office.

"There better not be any more issues after the Hot Chocolate catastrophe," Tevi yelled back to Mary.

Fortunately, the day was relatively calm, given everything that had happened. Even Sloan seemed to have recovered from the disastrous day. He made an announcement at the managers meeting that he had lost 10 pounds in the past month and was ready for anything. Sales for the day were moderate and customer issues were at a minimum.

Little did anyone realize; things were about to change for the employees of the HeidtMoore in a major way.

A few days later, Mary was headed to work. Olga had talked Mary into buying a new Fendi wrap dress which Mary was now wearing and feeling like a million dollars. It was a crisp, sunny December day. Her relationship with Nacho was #lit. And it seemed several other co-workers were beginning to feel the spirit of the holidays.

191

Since Brandi's return back to work, Mary had noticed a difference in her demeanor. Gone was the sparkly pink Yeti cup and the days where Brandi was more about the store gossip. Recently, she had been more focused, more in control, more.... *serious*. This was a Brandi Mary did not recognize, but she liked what she saw. They both had had more constructive conversations about Mary being promoted again and she was feeling positive about advancement. Today Mary would meet with her again first thing to talk about a potential job at corporate.

Before reaching the store, she stopped at Starbucks to get herself and Brandi a latte and a cappuccino. Just a nice little surprise for their meeting.

As she was walking towards the employee entrance, she passed the front of the HeidtMoore.

The doors were closed, padlocked shut.

Mary couldn't believe her eyes. Giant gold chains covered the gold doors to the store. The large windows were boarded up with plywood. *Had an animal escaped?* Mary didn't know what was going on.

Mary almost dropped both her drinks upon seeing the façade. She stood there. Gazing up at the large, overbearing gold sign that read "EIDTMOORE". The "H" was missing. A sense of panic, dread, despair shot through Mary like a sharp arrow.

She put the drinks down and dug into her Dior handbag to find her work phone. She called T. But all she got was a busy signal. She then tried Tevi, but she received the same busy signal. She then tried Nacho, Boggs and Sloan but had absolutely no luck getting through. Had the HeidtMoore turned off the work phones? She dug back in her bag, trying to find her personal phone, but she had left that at home. What was going on? This was like the Twilight Zone.

Approaching the heavily locked doors, Mary tried to open the doors, as if this were some mistake or a practical joke, and the chains, locks and metal bars were actually fake. They remained sealed. Mary looked to see if there was anyone around, any other employees who were trying to come to work, just as she was? Any other associates who were just as clueless as she was about why the store was sealed shut.

Had the HeidtMoore closed its doors for good? Only time would tell...

NO WAY OUT

COMING SOON!

The third book in the HeidtMoore series illustrates the retail profession even more and proves once you work in retail there really is *No Way Out.*

Follow us on Instagram and Facebook @heidtmoore

#personalappearancesareeverything

#onlineoroff

#nowayout

Made in the USA
Columbia, SC
15 November 2020